THE HOUSE OF THE FIFERS

THE HOUSE OF THE FIFERS

by

REBECCA CAUDILL

Decorations by Genia

LONGMANS, GREEN AND CO.
NEW YORK · LONDON · TORONTO
1954

27425
4/13/55

LONGMANS, GREEN AND CO., INC.
55 FIFTH AVENUE, NEW YORK 3

LONGMANS, GREEN AND CO. LTD.
6 & 7 CLIFFORD STREET, LONDON W 1

LONGMANS, GREEN AND CO.
20 CRANFIELD ROAD, TORONTO 16

THE HOUSE OF THE FIFERS

COPYRIGHT · 1954

BY REBECCA CAUDILL

PUBLISHED SIMULTANEOUSLY IN THE DOMINION OF CANADA BY
LONGMANS, GREEN AND CO., TORONTO

FIRST EDITION, APRIL, 1954
REPRINTED NOVEMBER, 1954

LIBRARY OF CONGRESS CATALOG CARD NUMBER 54-7564

Printed in the United States of America

For
CAPPIE AND EBERLEY
whose ancestral house
offered summer sanctuary to many a
niece and nephew

Contents

Contents

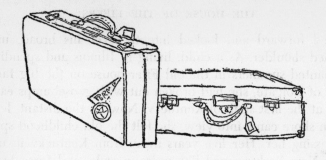

CHAPTER ONE

Reluctant Journey

As the big blue-and-chrome bus, scheduled for Paducah, nosed its way out of the Evansville bus station on a hot Saturday afternoon in early June, Monica Fifer waved a dutiful good-by to an elderly woman on the platform, and settled back in her seat to watch the city slip by.

Monica felt only annoyance that Aunt Willa Fifer had asked the woman to meet her at the train, and to put her on the bus for Colgate. Didn't Aunt Willa know that a fifteen-year-old girl from the city could find her way around without the help of sweet old ladies? Maybe Aunt Willa was expecting her to arrive in Colgate no older than when she had last left there—ten. Come to think of it, that seemed to be the age that her father was hoping a summer in the old Fifer house would turn her back to—ten. Monica bit her lip defiantly at the thought.

Within a matter of minutes, the bus left the business district behind, and turned on to the broad thoroughfare skirting the Ohio River. Monica, seated behind the driver, leaned forward and looked intently over his broad, uniformed shoulder. As a child, living in Illinois and spending enchanted summers in the old Fifer house on the big farm west of Colgate, she had broken out with goosebumps each year at the first sight of Kentucky. Now, as the distant, low, green shore came into view, she felt the old childhood spell possessing her. Her five years away from Kentucky in upstate New York seemed like years in exile, and for a brief moment her heart beat fast in anticipation.

"You going to Paducah?"

The thin, inquisitive voice of the passenger occupying the window seat beside Monica shattered the spell. She glanced at her questioner, a little bespectacled, pink-domed man nervously caressing the head of his cane.

It came over her suddenly that too many people during the last few months had made it their business to pry into her private affairs, and to shuffle them to suit themselves.

"I'm going to Colgate," she informed the man. "But," she added with frankness, "it wasn't my idea."

"Oh?" he said, with an invitation in his voice to explain herself. But Monica, preferring the company of her own thoughts, turbulent though they were, leaned back in her seat and ignored the invitation.

She wondered what changes five years would have brought to the old Fifer house and to the people living in it—to Uncle Steve and Aunt Willa, to her cousins, Harlan and Nancy and Doak.

The thought of Uncle Steve chastened her, now that she was soon to see for herself the changes in him that Aunt Willa had been describing in her letters to Monica's father. Uncle Steve, as she had known him during her summers on the Fifer farm, was compounded of energy that never flagged nor failed, and of good nature that never ran dry. In seasons of corn planting and haying and wheat harvest, he went lickety-split from pre-dawn until after dark, with the speed and efficiency of his well-kept combine and rotary plow and hay baler. Like the chimes of a dependable clock that regulate a household, his boisterous, hearty laugh sent out a deep-ringing tone by which the Fifer household kept its feelings in good order. No one, Monica remembered with swift affection, could be grumpy around Uncle Steve, nor grouchy, nor touchy.

Now Uncle Steve was crippled with arthritis. For two years, since its onset, the crippling had marched boldly through Uncle Steve's joints, and no offering of medical science had been able to appease it. Fortunately, it seemed arrested now, Aunt Willa wrote, but Uncle Steve no longer plowed the fields, nor baled the hay, nor combined the wheat. Instead, he rolled himself about the house and the lawn in a wheel chair or dragged himself from room to room on crutches.

Monica wondered if arthritis had crippled his cheerful disposition, too. She shuddered as she thought of the Fifer household without Uncle Steve's good nature to steer it.

Regardless of the changes in Uncle Steve, she knew Aunt Willa would not have changed. Aunt Willa was made of changeless, non-fading, non-shrinkable fabric. Let the sun shine, or let a storm blow up outside or inside the house, and Aunt Willa moved quietly, spoke calmly, and, in some mysterious way beyond childish fathoming, fathomed children's minds. At that moment, Monica found it hard to forgive her aunt's part in her father's conspiracy against her. But the recollection of meals in the Fifer house offset that grudge in part, at least. The prospect of Aunt Willa's sassafras-cured ham, her golden, fluffy, puffy cheese souffles, her hot biscuits and blackberry jam, her richly meringued chocolate pies, and her fresh peach ice cream had been one of the few compensations Monica had found in the summer's arrangements. She hoped Nancy had taken over no part of the cooking.

It was in her cousins that change would be most marked, Monica decided. Doak was one year old when Monica last spent a summer in Kentucky. He couldn't walk, or talk. Now, Monica calculated, he was transformed into a schoolboy. And if he was the kind of busy, busy bee Nancy's letters revealed herself to be, he was no doubt driving the tractor for Harlan on Saturdays and feeding blue-ribbon calves in his cops-and-robbers time.

In those earlier, happier summers, Harlan, nine years older than Monica, had been a big cousin to idolize, to tease about his girl friends, to play jokes on, and to hide things from. Now Harlan was married to Coralie Lang. He no longer lived in the big old house of the Fifers but in a new house across the rolling fields. When it was evident that Uncle Steve could no longer carry on, Harlan had left the university and returned home. Fortunately, he took to farming like a bird to air, and Uncle Steve, proud of him as a bantam hen of a lone chicken, rested easy in Harlan's planning and his judgment. Harlan had big plans afoot for the farm, Aunt Willa wrote. And he was certainly making things hum with all the new ideas he had brought from ag college, although, she added in her characteristic way, sometimes she was afraid for Harlan. He was in too much of a hurry.

It was Nancy, however, who in Monica's opinion must have changed the most. She and Nancy were the same age—fifteen. That last carefree summer they were together when they were ten seemed to Monica an interlude of complete charm to be cut off from time and treasured, as a girl keeps and treasures a long-loved doll. There had been chores to do, of course, as on all farms. Monica could even then hear Aunt Willa calling:

"Nancy, time for you and Monica to gather eggs now" . . . "Monica, suppose you and Nancy bring in the clothes now. Fold the sheets smoothly, girls" . . . "Girls, some lemonade would taste mighty good to the menfolks. Combining wheat is such a hot job. Would you like to make a jugful and take it to them? You may ride Firefly."

But when the chores were finished, theirs was a delightful freedom to do as they pleased. Sometimes they saddled Firefly, the gentlest—and slowest—of mares, and went for a jog up Leary's Hill under the cool arch of honey-locust trees. Sometimes they fished for long, lazy hours in the pond back of the barn, or, after a swim in the cool water, climbed on the raft anchored in the middle of the pond and stretched their dripping bodies full-length to dry in the sun.

Sometimes—a smile spread over Monica's face as she remembered—they busied themselves with their duties in the Firefly Club. The Club had been one of Nancy's many ideas. Only the two of them and their cousin Corcoran Fifer belonged, and they were all Club officials. Corky, as Keeper of the Steed, was the most important official, partly because he was the oldest, and partly because he refused to belong if he couldn't be Keeper of the Steed. Monica, as Keeper of the Trappings, dusted the saddle morning and evening, polished the bridle bits, and mended holes in the saddle blanket. Nancy, as Keeper of the Stable, swept out Firefly's stall every day, cleaned her feedbox, and plastered the walls of her stall with pictures—mountain scenes from discarded calendars and pastoral scenes from the covers of farm magazines.

Nancy had been such fun in those days when they were ten, Monica reflected with a sigh. Since then a thing called 4-H had come into her life, and her world, according to her letters, revolved with deadly seriousness around chickens and gardens, baby beeves and room improvement, sewing and cooking and reupholstering old chairs, and the prizes she had won for devotion to these pursuits. As more and more space in Nancy's letters had been given over to these activities, Monica had groaned with boredom. At fourteen, their letters had become thin and infrequent. At fifteen they had stopped altogether. Why spend time, argued Monica, writing letters to somebody who wrote in an unknown tongue?

"Do you by any chance live in Colgate?" Monica turned suddenly to the little old man riding beside her.

"Me? Oh, no. No." He shook his head vigorously. "I live a little ways beyond. Marion."

"Do you know anybody in Colgate?"

"Colgate? Why, yes. Yes, as a matter of fact, I do."

"Do you know the Fifers?"

"Steve Fifer?"

"That's the one."

"Sure. I know Steve Fifer mighty well."

"He's my uncle."

"You don't say!" exclaimed the man. He turned and beamed on her. "Mighty fine family, the Fifers, mighty fine folks."

"Yes, I know," said Monica. "That's why I'm going to visit them. They're supposed to be fine for what ails me."

"You? Something ailing you?"

The old man chuckled as he studied the girl beside him.

She wasn't pretty in the way a magazine-cover model is pretty. Her nose tilted upward a little too perkily for that, and her upper lip was a trifle long. Nevertheless, people had a way of looking at her twice. She was tall and slim, and she sat with easy grace in her reclining chair. Her complexion was as clean and fresh as snowy clothes hung to dry on a windy wash day; her short, upswept, light-brown hair glowed with golden tints, and her eyes were as blue as ageratum. But rebellion and restlessness were at work on her face.

"You?" the man repeated.

"I," said Monica. "My particular sins that brought on this trip to Kentucky," she confided to the stranger, "were riding around in a red convertible belonging to my friend Mimi Parry, and a freshman report card full of C's and D's. And I still think the punishment too heavy." Then, as abruptly as she had begun the conversation, she brought it to a close. Opening the magazine that lay on her lap, she pretended to read. But the lines blurred before her eyes as she thought of the bleak summer ahead of her. At least, she reflected, Corky would be there to suffer with her.

Corcoran Fifer lived in Knoxville. His summers, like Monica's earlier ones, were spent on the old Fifer farm where his father, and Monica's, had grown up along with Uncle Steve and Uncle Tom. Corky was eighteen now. Monica hadn't seen him since he was thirteen. That last summer they were together in the Fifer house, he had proved to be a pest to Monica and Nancy, prying into their secrets and telling them, and, whenever he thought he was evading the all-seeing eyes of Aunt Willa, running out on his household chores.

"He'll grow up some day," Aunt Willa always defended

him whenever Monica and Nancy complained. "For some reason, boys always need a little extra time to grow up."

According to all reports, Corky had not only grown up; he had grown up handsomely. The graduation picture Monica's father had received made Mimi Parry set an all-time record for raving. Corky had Monica's coloring and an athletic build, and he was easy to rave about. Not only was he the school's basketball hero but it was reported he had an unbroken string of A's on his report card. Sometime during his high-school days he had been elected president of almost every organization that rated in the school. He was entering Princeton in the fall on a scholarship, with plans to study law and later to go into politics. Corky, Monica decided, would be wasting his summer on the Fifer farm among the mules and pigs and chickens, and Corky was one Fifer who had brains enough to know it.

Besides Corky, there would be Benny, Uncle Tom's little boy, from Madisonville. Monica had never seen Benny. He was six, the age of Doak. He was too young, Monica decided, to fling much weight in any direction except that he would have to be fed, and his clothes would have to be washed and ironed by somebody, and that somebody might turn out to be Monica Fifer. She took an instant dislike to Benny Fifer. He was surplus population, she decided.

"Your daddy—" The man beside Monica wrinkled his forehead as he pieced together fragments of recollection. "Is your daddy Abbott Fifer?"

"Yes," answered Monica.

"Your mother—she was killed in an automobile wreck, wasn't she, a few years back?"

"Four years ago," Monica nodded.

"I recollect now reading something about that in the papers," said the man. "Your daddy married again?"

Monica turned on him. "Of course not!" she bristled. "That would be terrible."

"Well," mused the man, tilting his head sidewise, "there's no law against it. It's done every day."

Monica returned to her magazine, and to her private thoughts. From the day her mother was killed, Abbott Fifer had been both mother and father to her. He had found a tight-mouthed, vinegar-souled housekeeper whom he paid well to keep the house in order, to serve good meals on time, to keep clothes clean and socks darned. The things that couldn't be bought for his child with money—affection, and understanding, and companionship to fill the bewildering emptiness—he had tried to supply himself. He had arranged his business and his business contacts so that his time between five in the evening and eight in the morning belonged to Monica, and for three of the four years since Mrs. Fifer's death, their companionship had been the talk and envy of all her friends. He had been the life of Monica's parties, and, in their hours of comradeship, he had been a wise and witty and kindly guide through the maze of youth.

When Monica had entered high school, a change had come over Abbott Fifer. Monica couldn't understand him, and he certainly didn't understand her. He had got some rock-ribbed notions about her friend, Mimi Parry, and the oftener Mimi drove up in front of the Abbott Fifer house in her red convertible, and with her bright-colored scarf flying in the wind, the more set her father's notions had become.

As critical as she tried to be, however, Monica could see nothing really wrong with Mimi. Different, yes, but not wrong. What was wrong with Mimi's wearing expensively tailored clothes to school if that was the kind her family bought for her to wear? What was wrong with her bright-red lipstick? And with the bleached streak in her hair? And with smoking? And with carrying a key to her own front door, with which she could let herself in without waking the family? What was wrong with owning a convertible if her father wanted to give it to her, and what was wrong with driving it? Mimi, in her third year in high school, was two years older than Monica. She had a special junior permit to drive a car, and she was a good driver. Just because she had taken a liking to Monica the first day of school, and because she was generous and included a freshman when she was filling up the convertible with junior boys and girls—well, what was wrong with being kind to a freshman? Was it a crime to be generous, to love life, and fun, and football, and dances? Her father, Monica sometimes felt, seemed to think so.

He had laughed off the first few times Mimi stopped in front of the Fifer house and let Monica out of the crowded back seat of the convertible late for supper. He had laughed off the first few times Monica bolted her food to go to a swimming party, or on a hayride, or to one of Mimi's innumerable slumber parties. He had even joked when the silvery honk of Mimi's convertible called Monica away from a book he was trying to read to her.

After a month, however, he had begun to ask questions—prying, probing questions that made him appear gray-bearded and grandfatherly. Why couldn't a girl be home to supper on time? What about being quiet for just ten minutes, and studying her lessons? She did have lessons to study, didn't she? Did she have to drool on the telephone every single minute she was home? He was considering limiting her calls to one hour an evening, he said. And those boogie-woogie, be-bop, lovesick records she listened to all the time—couldn't she listen to a Beethoven symphony just once in a while? Once a month, say?

Monica had pleaded with him. She was no longer a child. She was in high school, in a big, new, exciting world where life was cut to a different pattern—oh, a very different pattern from the one he knew. Did he want her to be different from all her friends? If so, she soon wouldn't have any friends. Was that what he wanted?

A period had followed, Monica recalled, when her father seemed always to be thinking things but never saying them. Then, one day in February, she had brought home a report card loaded with C's and D's. That night while the telephone rang unanswered, he had demanded that she sit and listen to him. One statement of his broke through her rebellion like a dreadful clap of thunder.

"I'm writing your Aunt Willa tonight to ask if you may go down for the summer."

Monica had protested, at first calmly, then tearfully, as she sensed what a summer away from home would mean—away from Mimi, away from all her other friends and their gay round of parties and picnics, on a farm with Nancy and her calves, her garden, and all her good works.

Not even a sprinkling of B's on Monica's midterm report in early April had softened Abbott Fifer's heart. One evening in May he brought down her mother's big suitcase from the attic and told her she had better begin packing. Three evenings ago, the day before school ended, he had come home with her train ticket to Evansville.

As Monica watched the rolling Kentucky fields slip by, she relived that particular evening briefly.

"Monica, my child," she could hear her father saying, "somewhere along the way you've taken the wrong turning. It's because I want you back on the right road more than I want anything else in the world that I'm sending you to your Aunt Willa and the old house of the Fifers for the summer."

"You want me to be like Nancy, I suppose?" she had said, in rebellion and in bitterness.

"No, my child," he had answered. "I want you to be like Monica. I could ask nothing better than that. But I do ask that."

There had been a tenderness in his voice like a cooling salve that had soothed her bitterness, but it had not made any clearer to her what was expected of her.

"You're expecting a barnlot full of bawling calves and dirty, squealing pigs and kicking mules to make me like Monica? Is that it?" she had asked, her blue eyes brimming with tears.

"I'm expecting you to make yourself like Monica," he had said. "And I'm expecting the house of the Fifers to help you."

Tears blurred Monica's vision now as the bus rolled through Morganfield. A few minutes and a few miles later, familiar landmarks began to appear—the junction of the highway and the railroad where Uncle Steve had once flagged the five-o'-clock-in-the-morning accommodation train to Madisonville when she and Nancy were going to visit Uncle Tom; Miss Hattie Harper's apple orchard fanning out in orderly rows over its three long hills; the big, gray water tower of Colgate.

At sight of the water tower, a lump swelled in Monica's throat. What was it her father wanted of her, she wondered, desperate. To be arriving was like being pushed out on the stage to play a role, ignorant of part and words.

As the bus came to a stop in front of a filling station, Monica took a deep breath, stepped down into the aisle, and through the window searched the knot of waiting people for a familiar Fifer face.

CHAPTER TWO

The Return of the Prodigal

Hardly had Monica set foot on the ground when Nancy's arms were flung about her in a warm, tight hug.

"Monica!" cried Nancy. Then, relaxing her hold, she said accusingly, "You've been so long coming back!"

Momentarily Monica's dread scurried away in the warmth of the welcome, and in the memory of Nancy's generosity and her sincerity that had marked all their yesterdays.

"Yes," she laughed weakly, "I guess I have."

For a second, as people pushed their way past them, Monica studied her cousin. Nancy's brown eyes sparkled merrily. Short dark hair waved naturally about her face, and a glowing tan, set off by a red T-shirt and crisp white shorts, as naturally covered her body. She was inches shorter than Monica, slight and trim, with no waste. And, calculated Monica, suddenly remembering the blue ribbons that were reported to decorate Nancy's room, there was no waste of

14

her time, either. Every shining minute was undoubtedly filled to the brim.

"Here, give me your things," Nancy commanded. She relieved Monica of a small package and the magazine she was carrying, and grasped the handle of the heavy suitcase the driver had dragged from the baggage compartment. Starting across the street, she announced, "There's Mom beside the car."

"How you have grown up, my dear!" declared Aunt Willa as she embraced Monica. Then, holding her at arm's length and studying her, she added, "How handsomely you have grown up! I see a great deal has happened in five years."

"I guess something is bound to happen in five years." Monica laughed. Aunt Willa, she supposed, had been well briefed concerning the things that had happened to her.

She moved to help with her baggage, but Nancy had stowed away her possessions and slammed the trunk lid before she could offer assistance.

"Is your father well, Monica?" asked Aunt Willa.

"Yes, thank you," said Monica. "He's looking forward to a nice, quiet summer without me."

"And we're looking forward to a nice, jolly summer with you," Aunt Willa assured her. The warmth in her voice and the kindness in her gray eyes put to flight a portion of Monica's fears.

"Doak!" called Nancy. "Benny! Time to go!"

At Nancy's summons, two small boys, whom Monica had not noticed among the people waiting for the bus, edged reluctantly away from the crowd. With their hands deep in the pockets of their jeans, and with backward glances at the bus, they crossed the street to the car.

"Which one is Doak?" asked Monica.

A smile across the broad, freckled face of the taller boy flashed Monica a belated welcome. "I'm Doak."

"Hi-ya, Doak," said Monica.

"Hi!" he grinned.

"You must be Benny," said Monica, turning to the other boy, a slighter, smaller child with soft, questioning brown eyes set in a dark, oval face.

"Um-hum," said Benny, soberly.

"What say, Benny?" Monica held out her hand to him. He took it, but divided his attention between her and the bus, with the lion's share, Monica calculated, going to the bus.

"Monica, you don't mind sitting in the back seat with Doak and Benny, do you?" asked Nancy as she slid under the steering wheel.

Monica obediently climbed into the back seat of the car from one side while the boys crowded in from the other. In a flare of resentment she counted the orders Nancy had given in the five minutes since the bus had arrived. She would be taking orders from Nancy all summer, she supposed.

"Nancy has her learner's license," explained Aunt Willa as she settled herself in the front seat beside Nancy.

"Shucks, man! She can drive real good," spoke up Doak.

"But Aunt Willa has to sit in the front seat with her," added Benny. "The law says you have to sit there, doesn't it, Aunt Willa?"

Monica felt herself warming toward Benny.

"Till I'm sixteen," added Nancy. "Then I can get a driver's license."

Expertly Nancy backed the car into the street and headed it west in the direction of the Fifer farm.

"Tell us about your trip, Monica," invited Aunt Willa.

As Nancy drove the car down a residential street, deserted in the late afternoon heat, past the familiar old red-brick high school, past the coal yards, across the railroad tracks, past the White Front grocery on the edge of town, and out along the highway flanked by open, rolling fields, Monica related briefly such small happenings as seemed worth telling.

"Hey, Monicky!" Benny interrupted after a while. "You ever see one of those fantail pigeons?" He fastened steady dark eyes on her. "One of those pouter pigeons?"

"I don't believe so," replied Monica, glad to talk of something else. "What about them?"

"Benny and I are going to get us a pair," spoke up Doak. "Shucks, man!" he sighed with fervor. "You ought to see 'em. Pure white. The whitest white you ever saw."

"Whiter than white," amended Benny solemnly.

"Where are you going to get them?" asked Monica, warmed by their confidence.

"Boy down on the river's got some," said Doak. "Wants a dollar apiece for 'em."

"In about a week we'll have money enough to buy 'em," calculated Benny. "Or maybe two weeks."

"I thought you lost your money, Benny," said Nancy. "Have you found it yet?"

"No," reported Benny. "I just can't remember where I laid that money down."

"Corky came Monday, Monica," announced Nancy.

"What's he doing now?" asked Monica, wondering why he had not been at the bus to meet her.

"He and Harlan are cultivating corn this afternoon," Nancy told her.

"Do the menfolks still work twenty hours a day, Aunt

Willa? Every day but Sunday?" asked Monica, remembering how Aunt Willa always waited supper until Uncle Steve and Harlan came from the fields, and how at the end of a stretched-out day everything seemed shoved together in one over-sized operation—supper, dishwashing, separating the cream, listening to Uncle Steve read from the Bible, and falling into bed already nine-tenths asleep. She wondered if Uncle Steve, now crippled with arthritis, still read from the Bible.

Aunt Willa's laughter broke in on her thoughts. "Did it seem as bad as that?" she asked.

"You still have to get up early and work late if you're going to keep up with Harlan," volunteered Nancy, with pride in her voice.

"Corky's a life saver," added Aunt Willa. "He not only helps Harlan in the fields, but he and Nancy between them do most of the chores."

"Maybe you'd like to help me with the milking, Monica, as one of your summer chores. That would give Corky more time to help Harlan."

"Well-ll," Monica hesitated, searching for a tempered way to refuse, "I don't suppose you've asked the cows about that?"

"Oh, Monica, you silly old thing!" Nancy laughed impulsively. "I'm so glad you've come!"

"Man, look at that!" Doak pointed to a cloud of yellow dust boiling up in the wake of a tractor in a roadside field.

"It hasn't rained here for eight weeks, Monica," Aunt Willa said. "We had one little shower early in April. Enough to make the corn come up. We haven't had a drop since."

"That's too bad," murmured Monica, sensing that the lack of rain was a tragedy she was expected to exclaim about.

Halfway up the next hill, Nancy turned the car off the main highway on to a graveled road—the Roller Coaster Road, Monica remembered they had called it because of its succession of small, steep hills. From the top of the second hill, the house of the Fifers came into view across the fields on a distant knoll.

At sight of it, Monica leaned forward.

Built by Monica's Great-great-grandfather Fifer, more than a hundred years ago, the house had sheltered five generations of Fifers. T-shaped and painted white, it stood with commanding dignity on its broad, sloping lawn shaded by the grove of silver maples Great-great-grandfather Fifer had transplanted there. Massive brick chimneys stood at each end of the house, providing fireplaces for spacious living rooms and for upstairs bedrooms as well. Across the front of the house, and along each side of the stem of the T, ran long, narrow porches, their ceilings supported by tall slender columns joined by glistening white scrollwork. The house, thought Monica, studying it from the distance, was like a belle of the olden days, wearing voluminous, stiffly starched petticoats with flounces of snowy eyelet embroidery. True, the belle was remarkably well preserved for her age, but the world had long ago passed her by. And what was to be gained from spending a summer in her company?

The road commanded a view of the front and the west porches. The front porch Monica and Nancy had named the Sociable Porch, for it was there that summer afternoon callers were entertained as they sat in the big swing or in the cushioned rocking chairs sipping lemonade and visiting with Aunt Willa.

The long west porch they had named the Kinfolks Porch. It also was furnished with a swing and rocking chairs, but seldom did anyone sit in them except Fifers. The Fifers were likely to gather there in the summer evenings, particularly when kinfolks came visiting. It was there that Aunt Willa sat in the swing in mid-morning to rest from the early morning chores while she strung beans for dinner. There Doak as a baby had played in his pen, and with unintelligible gibberish had greeted the menfolks as they came from the barn at milking time. There, late in the afternoons, Monica and Nancy had stretched out with their books, or played with their dolls, or with the current crop of kittens. And in the long summer twilights at harvest time, in the lull before supper, Monica remembered how Aunt Willa had sat looking contentedly out over the rolling green and golden hills as she waited for the menfolks to come home from the fields.

The east porch, which Monica couldn't see from the road, she and Nancy had named Bridget's Porch, after a maid-of-all-work in a story. It was wider and more spacious than the others, and it was screened. Its furniture was a washing machine and an ironing board, broad shelves on which tomatoes were spread to ripen in the morning sun and milk buckets were placed upside down to air, a workbench, and a cupboard whose doors were shut on almost every conceivable housewife's tool from a scrub mop to an ice pick. Monica remembered that old raincoats, an umbrella, and broad-brimmed straw hats hung along the south wall, handy insurance against any kind of weather. At the end of the porch, away from the kitchen, were two cots where she remembered she and Nancy had often slept during the hot summer months.

"Who sleeps on Bridget's Porch this summer?" she asked.

"We do," Benny and Doak answered her.

South of the house, in the distance, was a range of hilly

pasture land on which grazed a herd of white-faced Hereford cattle. Directly back of the house were chicken lots, shaded by a giant cottonwood tree, where Aunt Willa's big flock of white Plymouth Rock hens were being coaxed into laying by the latest scientific theories.

"Who gathers the eggs now, Aunt Willa?" asked Monica, remembering her childish satisfaction at transferring warm eggs from nest to basket.

"These are my right-hand men now," said Aunt Willa, glancing fondly at Doak and Benny.

"Benny's scared of the setting hens," announced Doak.

"So was I, Benny," Monica assured him.

"Shucks, man, they sure can peck!" declared Doak.

"They peck to kill," amended Benny solemnly.

At the Fifer mailbox, Nancy turned the car off the graveled road into the private lane that marked the last lap of Monica's journey. Monica felt like a culprit being escorted to prison for three months. Up another hill, past the house where one of the hired men lived, down the hill, and across a narrow bridge they rolled. There they turned sharply, went through the big gate, past the barn, and up the final hill to the house.

"Here's your Uncle Steve, Monica, waiting for you," announced Aunt Willa, as Nancy brought the car to a stop in front of the gate and everyone began climbing out.

A lump rose in Monica's throat as she caught sight of Uncle Steve sitting in his wheel chair under one of the maples. The newspaper he had been reading had fallen to the ground. He was leaning forward in his chair, waiting, and the light of good nature in his face, Monica saw with relief, was not one whit dimmed.

"Well, well, if it isn't *Miss* Fifer, all grown up and pretty

as a picture!" Uncle Steve's hearty voice boomed a welcome.
"Come here, child," and he opened his arms to embrace her.

Tears dimmed her eyes as she kissed Uncle Steve's cheek
and felt his arms lovingly about her. How changed he was,
she thought, and how unchanged!

The others joined them, dropping down into the rustic
chairs in the shade of the maples.

"How was your driving today, Nancy?" Uncle Steve asked.

"Fine!" reported Nancy. "I did a perfect parking job at the
bus station. The best one yet." She launched into a play-by-
play description of her trip into town and home again, a
recital that seemed to Monica tiresomely detailed.

"The bus was going to Paducah," Doak told Uncle Steve.

"Farther than that," said Benny. "To the Pacific Ocean,
maybe."

Uncle Steve laughed heartily. "These two, Monica," he
said, "I call Plain and Fancy. They make a good team. One
of them has his feet on the ground, and the other has his head
in the clouds. And now let's hear from you. When a fellow's
sort of planted in one spot the way I am, he has to depend on
other people's ears and eyes, you know."

Hastily Monica searched among her travel experiences for
something to report, but she could recall little except that
she had loathed coming, and the loathing had hidden all incidents of importance or of no importance alike under a thick
film as of dust.

"On the bus I sat beside a man from Marion who knows
you," she reported.

"That so? What was his name?"

"I don't know," she said. "We talked only a little. And
your friend met me in Evansville, Aunt Willa. Mrs.—what
was her name?"

"Mrs. Smith," supplied Aunt Willa. "I'm glad. I always think it lets you down to arrive some place and find nobody there to welcome you." She turned to Uncle Steve. "John Jarvis was plowing his corn as we came by. The ground is so dry it makes you hurt for all the things depending on it."

Then, suddenly, as if to erase what she had just said, Aunt Willa rose from her chair and started into the house. "We'd better get at the chores, children."

The spacious old house, mellow in the June sunset, and resting peacefully, jerked itself to life as the Fifers entered.

"Doak," suggested Aunt Willa, "you can pump water for the chickens, and Benny can bring feed from the shed. Nancy, you bring your father's chair in the house before you start supper, will you? And Monica," Aunt Willa paused as she looked kindly at her, "you find your way around, my dear, and take your time about getting used to us."

"How about the milking, Mother?" asked Nancy. "Aren't Monica and I going to do the milking?"

"Let Monica get her bearings first, child. After five long years that takes a little time. Corky will help you tonight. Monday will be time enough to enroll Monica in all your projects."

"Maybe I'll go outside and talk with Uncle Steve awhile," suggested Monica, feeling unashamedly grateful that Uncle Steve's helplessness and his need for companionship might provide an escape from Nancy's projects.

"I believe he's already coming in, Monica," said Aunt Willa. "He's a kitchen maid now. He's wonderful help about the house."

Monica, hearing a footfall on the Kinfolks Porch, turned to see Uncle Steve dragging himself along toward the kitchen door on his crutches. Nancy ran quickly to pull his chair up the steps.

When Aunt Willa and the boys had gone to the chicken houses, laden with buckets of mash and pails of water, and baskets for eggs, Nancy brought potatoes for Uncle Steve to peel, and put water on the gas stove to boil. Monica stood in the doorway watching her.

"You do the cooking now?" she asked skeptically.

"I help," said Nancy. "Learning to cook was one of my 4-H projects. But I like my livestock projects better than cooking."

"Wait till you see T-Bone, Monica," said Uncle Steve proudly.

"And who, may I ask, is T-Bone?" asked Monica, suspicious.

"T-Bone's the baby beef I'm going to show this summer," explained Nancy. "He's part of my meal ticket through college."

Monica groaned inwardly. "Maybe I'd better begin unpacking," she said.

"Don't start till I get the potatoes on," begged Nancy. "I want to go up with you."

"Nancy's got something she wants to show you, Monica," explained Uncle Steve.

Monica watched as Uncle Steve peeled the potatoes. His fingers were stiff, and he held the peeler awkwardly. It reminded her of the awkwardness with which she and Nancy had peeled potatoes when they were eight and nine. She hadn't peeled a potato since her mother died. That was one of the benefits of having an efficient housekeeper who didn't tolerate a youngster underfoot, she reflected. It relieved her of peeling potatoes.

"Put the plates on the table for me now, Nancy," said Uncle Steve as Nancy poured boiling water on the potatoes, "and the silver, and I'll set the table while you introduce Monica to your room."

A minute later, the girls started up the long flight of stairs to the room which Monica had always shared with Nancy. Nancy led the way, straining under the weight of Monica's suitcase, which she insisted on carrying. Monica trailed behind, carrying her small possessions. She wished she might have a room of her own, a place where she could withdraw from talk of plowing, milking, and fattening calves, and live her own private life. But wishing for that in the house of the Fifers was like wishing for the sun and the moon to exchange places. Whoever lived in the Fifer house shared. What was worse, Monica remembered, he was expected to share cheerfully.

At the head of the stairs, across the hallway from the room Corky occupied, Nancy pushed open the door of her room and stood aside for Monica to enter. Monica stumbled listlessly across the doorsill, but, once inside, she opened her eyes wide.

"You've—changed everything!" she declared.

"Do you like it?" asked Nancy eagerly. She was watching Monica with expectancy.

"Well," hesitated Monica, "it's such a big change—"

She looked about the room. The white metal bed with the slightly sagging springs that she remembered had been replaced with an old walnut spool bed with high posts at the four corners. A walnut dresser with heavy fruit-cluster handles on the drawers had replaced the vanity dresser. A quaint walnut desk stood near the south window. In the sunset glow, the old furniture, rubbed and polished to a gleaming satin, richly mirrored the enduring strength and charm of a by-gone day. A heavy ivory candlewick spread covered the bed. On the floor was a braided rag rug on which fell the evening light subdued by ruffled white curtains at the broad windows. On either side of the fireplace stood a big wing chair, chintz-covered, inviting a girl to curl up with a book. The walls of the low-ceilinged room were papered, soft ivory stripes alternating with old-fashioned nosegays of pink rosebuds. Over the mantel hung an oil portrait of a young girl. Judging by her appearance, she was not much older than Monica and Nancy, but her tight-fitting basque waist, her bustle, and the cut of her dark bangs dated her as belonging with the furniture.

"That's our Great-aunt Eugenia," Nancy introduced the girl in the portrait.

"Who was she?" asked Monica.

"She was the one who was killed when she fell from the horse. When she was seventeen. Just when she was about to be married. Remember, Grandma told us?"

"I'd forgotten, I guess. Where did you unearth her?"

"Among Great-grandma Fifer's old things piled up in the hayloft, of all places. Isn't she sweet?"

"Not bad," agreed Monica, somehow uneasy, as if the steady blue eyes in the portrait were passing judgment on her.

"How do you like the rest of the room?" asked Nancy. "The bed and the dresser belonged to Great-great grandma Fifer. Think of it! They're more than a hundred years old. The desk was made out of a little old organ that belonged to Great-grandma Fifer. And the chairs were Grandma's."

"Why did you go in for all this antique stuff?" asked Monica.

"Don't you like it?" Disappointment was in Nancy's voice.

"It's all right," said Monica. "But with all the pretty modern furniture you can get nowadays—"

"But this furniture belongs here," Nancy protested. "The pieces are all part of this house. Part of its past."

When Monica failed to reply, Nancy walked across the room and opened one of the dresser drawers. "These two top drawers are yours," she said. "And half the closet. I'll run down and get along with supper while you unpack."

At the doorway she turned and surveyed the room lovingly. "It took me two years to do this room," she said.

"What do you mean, you?" asked Monica.

"I did it," answered Nancy simply. "With just a little help from Dad, and a little from Mom, and a lot from Corky on the desk. It was a 4-H project. This room was the thing that won me a trip to Washington. Don't you remember I wrote you about that?"

"Did you?" asked Monica. "Maybe I didn't get the letter. I didn't know you'd been to Washington."

"That's a long story I'll have to tell you, chapter by chapter," declared Nancy, "and illustrate it with my scrapbook. All my expenses paid. Shook hands with the President. Everything. Hurry, now. See you in the kitchen."

As soon as Nancy had gone, Monica softly shut the door behind her, and sank down into one of the wing chairs. She wished with all her heart that she was back at home. She felt frightened and unhappy. Great-aunt Eugenia's deep-blue eyes looking straight at her from the portrait did nothing to reassure her. All right, she admitted defiantly to Eugenia, the room was beautiful. Of course, Nancy was a seven-days' wonder to have done it all by herself. Of course, she deserved a trip to Washington, and a chance to shake the President's hand. But what of it? What had that to do with Monica?

After a while, when she had faced the fact that nothing was to be gained by sitting there, she forced herself out of the chair, opened her suitcase, and transferred her possessions to closet and dresser drawers. Then, with a well-aimed kick she landed her suitcase under the bed, and went slowly downstairs and out on the Kinfolks Porch.

"All settled?"

"That you, Aunt Willa?" Monica called, peeping into the kitchen.

"Come on in," invited Aunt Willa. "Nancy's gone to milk and look after T-Bone. Did you find everything you need upstairs?"

"Yes," said Monica, entering the kitchen, "but I feel like a fish out of water in that room."

"You'll get used to it," Aunt Willa reassured her. "Nancy's been anxious for you to see it."

Aunt Willa was cutting thick slices off a roasted ham. "Would you like to pour milk?" she asked.

When Monica had poured the milk, and, at Aunt Willa's request, had brought applesauce and strawberry jam from the fruit cellar, she retreated again to the Kinfolks Porch. From the swing she watched a bright-red tractor come bounding over the Roller Coaster Road with Corky in the seat.

"Hey, Doak!" Corky shouted a moment later from the barnyard as he climbed down from the tractor seat. "Milking time! Benny!"

Doak and Benny appeared from the back of the house and went racing to the barn. While Corky and Nancy milked, the boys opened the corral gate a crack and turned hungry calves into the barnyard with the cows, and later shoved them, well-fed, through the crack into the corral again, and between acts held the kittens' pan to be filled with warm milk.

Monica, watching and listening, wanted to go both to the barn and back into the house, as if magnets pulled her feet in both directions. In earlier summers she would have been at the barn, in the thick of the activity. Now she didn't fit in there. But she wasn't sorry, she told herself as she picked up a magazine. She didn't want to fit in.

As dusk settled, the Fifers came from the barn to the house, Doak and Benny in front, throwing pebbles at the cottonwood, Nancy and Corky behind, each carrying a bucket of milk. Monica's eyes were fastened on Corky as he crossed the yard to the Kinfolks Porch. He was good-looking even when he was covered with several layers of cornfield dust, she noticed.

"Hi, Corky!" she called, getting up from the swing.

He held out his free hand. "Well, well," he greeted her warmly. "So we got a new milk hand, huh? We could stand another."

Monica's shoulders wilted. She had counted Corky an ally, and he spoke the language of the other Fifers.

At the supper table Monica tried fitfully to make herself one of the Fifers. But she no sooner joined in the conversation than she found it veering off in directions she couldn't follow. Sometimes Aunt Willa or Uncle Steve asked her questions, but, when she had answered them, the conversation picked up where it had been interrupted, and that was worlds and eternities away from Mimi and her convertible and fun-packed schooldays. She watched Corky and listened hopefully for signs of dissatisfaction with his lot. But he ate enormous amounts of supper, discussed politics with Uncle Steve, talked T-Bone with Nancy, kidded Doak and Benny to their great delight, and seemed to have nothing to say to Monica.

As soon as he finished his dessert, he asked to be excused from the table. "Supper was larrupin', Aunt Willa," he said. "How about the car tonight, Uncle Steve?"

"Sure, Corky," said Uncle Steve. "Which girl is it tonight?"

"Corky, I thought maybe you'd take Monica and me to a show tonight," complained Nancy.

"Can't. Got a date. What's the matter with George Cole?"

"I told you George is working at Paducah this summer," explained Nancy.

Corky looked critically at Monica. "You ought to be able to land a boy friend," he said.

Half an hour later he went down the front walk, bathed and shaved, wearing gray flannels and a white shirt open at the neck. He was whistling.

As soon as dishwashing got under way, Monica felt the magnets pulling at her feet again. One pulled her to the kitchen where Nancy was washing dishes, with Uncle Steve drying, and Aunt Willa putting them away. The other pulled her to where Doak and Benny were shutting up the chickens for the night. She went to the chicken lot, but, instead of helping the boys shoo the chickens into the house, she dallied under the cottonwood tree, scuffing the toe of a shoe against the crotchety roots and fighting back her tears.

When finally the chores were finished and the Fifers were relaxing from their labors, Harlan and Coralie joined them on the Kinfolks Porch. They had dropped by to say hello to the stranger, they said. But after the greetings were finished, Harlan talked to Uncle Steve about the drought, and Coralie, whom Monica remembered as having eyes and ears for nothing but Harlan, discussed with Aunt Willa the best way to treat roupy chickens, and told how her tomatoes were shriveling in the dry wind and falling off the vines. Monica was glad when they went home.

"Benny, you and Doak still awake?" asked Uncle Steve.

"Yes, sir," they said, half asleep.

"Want us to roll you in, Uncle Steve?" asked Benny.

"Just my chair," said Uncle Steve. And after pulling himself slowly and painfully from the chair, he hobbled on his crutches to the living room. Quietly the others followed, and, seating themselves, waited.

Uncle Steve took the Bible and opened it. He had always read it just before bedtime. Abbott Fifer had read the Bible to Monica, too, but lately she had been too much in demand by Mimi to be present at reading time. She glanced at Aunt Willa, at Nancy and Doak and Benny. They all sat content, listening to Uncle Steve's clear, strong voice.

And he said, A certain man had two sons. And the younger of them said to his father, Father, give me the portion of goods that falleth to me. And he divided unto them his living.

Through the moving story of the son who had wasted his living and returned home penitent, Monica listened intently. The story stayed with her as she said good night and followed Nancy upstairs to bed. It stayed with her as she lay awake in the dark—the utter, strange dark of the open country, unlike the make-believe dark of cities—and heard dogs barking at some remote farmhouse, and cattle bawling on the hillsides.

She was a prodigal, too, she reflected. Judged by standards in the old Fifer house, she had wasted her living. She couldn't cook a meal, or polish up old furniture, or milk a cow. But, unlike the prodigal in the Bible, she didn't care. It was stupid of her father to think that by sending her here he could erase five years of her life and make her over. The prodigal son in the Bible had come crawling home to say how sorry he was, and to try to mend his ways and become like his elder brother, who was full of good works and had a mean, disagreeable disposition. Well, she was sorry for nothing, and Nancy Fifer was the last person in the world she wanted to be like.

"How long are those cattle going to keep up that bawling?" she asked impatiently.

"They're hungry, Monica," Nancy told her.

"Why doesn't somebody feed them then?"

"Didn't you hear us talking about the drought?" asked Nancy. "We told you it hasn't rained a single drop since early April. And the hot winds are like fire across the pastures."

CHAPTER THREE

Blue Monday

On Monday, the cattle awoke Monica in the early, indistinct dawn. Now one, now another expressed its hunger in a surly, raucous bawl that rifled the morning calm. The same complaints had awakened her on Sunday morning, too. She folded the pillow about her head in an effort to deaden the sound. If it was rain the cattle were bawling for, she wished with gritted teeth that the heavens would open and let them have it quickly.

There had been speculation at Sunday breakfast concerning the possibility of rain. Uncle Steve had told dramatic stories of rains that had broken other droughts. Corky, looking for hopeful forecasts, had produced an almanac that apparently scored a record for wrong guesses. Aunt Willa reported she had heard on the radio that rain had fallen in Indiana, and even in the next county there had been a light sprinkle. But as soon as breakfast was finished, the Fifers had stopped their speculation as if it were a game they had

33

been playing, and had flown at their preparations for Sunday school, just as Monica remembered they always had.

Monica had long ago given up Sunday school at home. It was a pastime for children, she had persuaded her father. But she couldn't persuade him to excuse her from church, not even when she had stayed awake all of the night before at one of Mimi's hilarious slumber parties.

She recalled yesterday's scramble as the Fifers had made ready for Sunday school. Aunt Willa had broken into the leisurely breakfast conversation with the warning, "Look at the time!" Immediately everybody had dashed to his post and started to work. While Corky had turned the ice cream freezer on Bridget's Porch, Uncle Steve had separated the cream, Nancy had made beds, Benny had reported period-ically that he still hadn't found his Sunday shoes, Doak had called what was he supposed to wear, and Aunt Willa had raced through the breakfast dishes, put a chicken to frying for Sunday dinner, and answered everybody's questions in an unruffled voice.

Monica had been viewing the orderly confusion from the safety of the dining room when Corky had caught sight of her. "Hey, Monica," he shouted above the hubbub, "don't you know there's a war on?"

"It isn't my war," she had told him with cool satisfaction.

He had stopped turning the freezer to look at her. "Well, I'll be darned!" was all he had said.

Nancy stirred in bed, and yawned.

Monica hastily marshaled her thoughts away from their excursions into yesterday, and faced the present and inescap-able facts of life in the house of the Fifers. This was Monday, she remembered. This was the day it had been planned that she should help with the milking.

"Dear me!" Nancy suddenly shot upright in bed. "It's time to get up."

"What time is it?" grumbled Monica.

"Six," answered Nancy.

"We didn't use to get up at this creepy hour," Monica told her, recalling that on earlier visits she and Nancy awoke leisurely and lay in bed watching on the wall the flowing, shifting shadows made by the play of the early morning sun and the breeze among the maples.

"Those days are gone forever," Nancy told her cheerfully, as she pulled a T-shirt over her head. "As long as we go to bed at a reasonable hour, it doesn't matter if we get up early. I have to get enough sleep, else my health chart doesn't bear inspection."

"Do you chart everything, Nancy?" asked Monica, recalling with boredom the scrapbook of the trip to Washington, the numerous 4-H record books, and project books, and charts, and graphs Nancy had thrust upon her in their free moments on Sunday afternoon. "You charted this room down to the last thumbtack. You chart your garden. You chart T-Bone. Now you're charting your sleep."

"It's important to keep records," said Nancy. "Else how do you know where you are? Or what you're doing? Or where you're going?"

Monica yawned. Some day, she thought, while Nancy was charting, life—dates and parties and dances and good times —was going to skip by her, and leave her a busy old maid.

For a moment she studied her cousin. What she saw, she had to admit, didn't exactly square with her forecast. Nancy was standing in front of the handsome old dresser, running a brush vigorously through her short dark hair and pushing the waves becomingly about her face. There was energy to burn in the lean, compact body, and Nancy burned it extravagantly, whether charting her daily doings, singing in the church choir, or, as pictures in her high-school year book proved, leading a pep parade at a football game. And the burning made a cheery fire that drew people to her as a street lamp draws moths.

"You're counting on me to help you milk, aren't you?" asked Monica.

"If you want to," said Nancy, still busy with her hair.

Thoughtfully she laid the brush down and turned to look at Monica.

"Of course, if you don't want to—if you'd rather not . . . It's just that if you took over the milking for Corky, he could be of more help to Harlan. And in the summer Harlan needs all the help he can get. It takes a lot of man-hours to carry out his programs."

Monica yawned again, stretched, and began timidly getting out of bed. She would at least score one on Corky if she took over the milking.

"I'll help," she announced. "When do we eat?"

"After we milk," said Nancy.

"I don't have to chart my milking, do I?" asked Monica.

Impulsively Nancy snatched up a pillow and threw it at Monica. "Silly!" she scoffed. "I don't believe you like us any more, Monica."

"I don't like the charts," Monica said frankly.

"Well, you don't have to keep 'em," Nancy assured her. "If you'll hurry, I'll wait for you."

Monica began half-heartedly to get into her blue jeans. "What's that noise I hear?"

"All sorts of things," said Nancy. "Mother getting breakfast. Daddy setting the table. Corky whistling on his way to the barn. Everybody's making noise but Doak and Benny. Mother lets them sleep till seven."

"Oh, to be Doak or Benny!" sighed Monica as she ran a comb through her hair.

"Ready?" asked Nancy.

She led the way down the stairs, and Monica stumbled after her. They took milk buckets from the shelf on Bridget's Porch, and set out down the hill, past the big cottonwood tree, toward the barn.

In the earlier summers, Monica had haunted the Fifer barnyard at the evening milking time. When she was four and five, she and Nancy had perched on the fence, watching. Later, when they had grown bigger and bolder, they had teased Uncle Steve and Harlan to allow them to milk, and had fed the meager results to the never-failing batch of new kittens. Following Nancy through the gate in the early morning light, however, with a milk bucket in her hand, she saw the barnyard as a deadly earnest place.

Everywhere was noise—loud and raucous and insistent noise—mules fighting at the water trough, hogs grunting, little pigs squealing, lambs bleating, chickens cackling, kittens mewing, dogs barking, cows and calves bawling, and Corky, high in the hayloft throwing down hay, whistling "Pharaoh's Army Got Drownded." The barnyard smells were as pronounced as the noises—the strong smell of many animals, the sweet smell of dry alfalfa, the acrid smell of the stalls.

"It—it kinda turns your stomach before breakfast," confided Monica, with a squeamish expression on her face.

"What does?" asked Nancy.

"This rare perfume."

"Oh," Nancy scoffed, "you'll soon get used to it."

The whistling in the hayloft stopped abruptly. "Hey!" called Corky from the dimness. "That you, Nancy?"

"Right," called Nancy.

"Got your helper with you?"

"Sure. She's right here."

"Monica," shouted Corky, "let's see some fancy milking now."

"You mind your business, Corky Fifer!" Monica shot at him.

"Did I hear a bee buzz by?" called Corky. And he went back to whistling cheerfully of the tragedy that befell Pharaoh's army.

"Which cow do you want me to milk?" asked Monica.

"Here's the gentlest one," said Nancy, singling out one of the six cows to be milked. "Suppose you begin on her."

Monica brought a milking stool from the stable shed, sat down at a respectful distance, and timidly pulled on a teat. The cow craned her neck to stare at the intrusion.

"Cows have terribly long necks, don't they?" Monica quavered, backing off and eying the situation critically. "Like giraffes."

Nancy, astraddle a milking stool, was milking furiously with both hands, the two streams of milk seesawing a steady tune in the foam they made.

"Go after it hard, Monica," she advised. "And put up a good bluff. A cow's terribly bent on business and won't take any foolishness. If she once finds out you're afraid, she'll make your life miserable."

"So, bossy!" quavered Monica. "I suspect she already knows the truth."

"Catch hold higher up, like this," Nancy advised, demonstrating the art of milking. It looked so absurdly easy the way Nancy did it.

Cautiously Monica tried and found it worked. The results weren't handsome, like Nancy's demonstration, but at least milk was coming steadily in a piddling stream.

"Now you're getting the hang of it," encouraged Nancy.

"How long does this go on?" asked Monica. Then, "Ow!" she shrieked, retreating hurriedly with the bucket as the cow struck the side of her head sharply with the bony part of her tail. "What did she do that for?"

"Just a fly," explained Nancy unconcernedly.

"Well, she needn't have been so thorough about it," complained Monica. "It doesn't take an atomic bomb to knock out a fly."

She swallowed hard and set her mouth grimly as she studied the intentions of the cow, which, apparently, had forgiven and forgotten. Cautiously she returned to the stool and began to milk again, at first timidly, gradually gaining confidence as the milk rose slowly in the bucket.

For a long time the cow chewed her cud and behaved like a well-contented lady. Then, "Ow! Nancy!" screamed Monica, as the cow, with no warning whatever, lifted a hind foot high, planted it squarely in the milk bucket, and departed, knocking Monica off the stool in passing, and upsetting the warm milk over her.

"Look what she's done now!" shrieked Monica, close to tears.

Nancy set her bucket aside and came running. "Did she hurt you, Monica?" she asked, bending over her and rescuing the bucket.

Monica rubbed her shins and wiggled her toes. The warm

milk made a squshy sound in her loafers, and her dripping blue jeans clung to her legs.

"No, I'm not hurt," she grumbled, getting up from the ground. "Not permanently, anyway. But, ugh! What a nice way to begin a vacation!"

"I'm sorry, Monica," declared Nancy. "That cow is usually as gentle as a kitten."

"Well, something or other has surely rubbed her fur the wrong way this morning," whined Monica. "You finish her and let me learn on yours."

"You'd better keep learning on the one you started on." Corky's voice startled the girls. They turned to see him standing in the doorway of the barn. Apparently he had witnessed the whole humiliating scene. Now he rounded up the ill-mannered cow and drove her back to Monica.

"If at first you don't succeed, Monica, try, try again," he advised.

"Don't quote poetry at me!" snapped Monica.

"Well, as poetry, it is pretty bad," he said. "But the sentiments are sound. Here. Hand me the bucket and let me wash it out."

In a moment he brought the bucket back from the pump and handed it to Monica. "I'll stand here to tell Bossy she must cease and desist if she starts straying again. Go to it, now."

"Well," said Monica, "if you've got time to stand, you've got time to milk." She thrust the bucket toward him.

"And what do you contribute?" asked Corky.

"Listen, Corky," Nancy interrupted, getting up from her stool. "I'll finish milking that cow. Monica can learn on mine."

"Well—" Corky scratched his head. "I don't think the summer's prospects are very promising. Here!" He held out his hand. "Give me that bucket, Monica. I'd better help Nancy with the milking."

"You go and whistle," advised Monica. "I'll show you I can milk."

"Great gal!" whooped Corky. And off he went toward the house, whistling more piercingly than ever about the fate of Pharaoh's army.

When he had gone, Monica sat down at a respectful distance from the cow Nancy had been milking, and in terror and anger set to work.

"Let your arms relax," Nancy advised. "Just forget yourself and feel friendly toward the cow."

"Is there such a thing as synthetic friendliness?" asked Monica. "Because I sure can't manufacture the genuine article."

Nancy laughed. "That'll come."

"Do you honestly feel friendly toward these cows?" Monica asked.

"Of course. They're not too different from people. They all have personalities. And they know when you like them and when you don't."

"Well, I guess they've got my number then. Because I don't give a hang for any of them."

Nancy stopped milking and looked at Monica, her face serious. "Had you rather not help with the milking?" she asked. "I thought—well, we always did everything together, and I just thought the summer would be fun if we—if we did things together the way we used to."

"But when we did things together before," argued Monica, "we did different kinds of things. We rode Firefly. And swam. And fished. And picnicked. We weren't so deadly serious about milking, and gardening, and—and charting."

"We were ten then," Nancy reminded her. "Now we're fifteen. We're grown up."

In silence, Monica pulled doggedly on the cow's teats.

"If you'd rather not help me—"

"I'll help," Monica replied sullenly, "if for no other reason than to show Corky I can."

"I don't think that's sufficient reason for helping," said Nancy.

"It'll do," snapped Monica, close to tears.

Harlan drove over the hill from his house and into the barnyard just as the milking was finished.

"Sure looks natural to see you around, Monica," he said.

He caught sight of the milk stains on her blue jeans. "Had a little trouble, huh?"

Monica glanced disgustedly at the gooey patch of milk on her jeans, and wiggled her toes in her wet, sticky loafers.

"I guess I wasn't cut out for a milkmaid."

"Shucks, now! Don't give up so easily."

He turned to Nancy. "Hear those cicadas?" he asked, shaking his head. "They're really wound up, aren't they? Bet it goes over a hundred ten in the shade today. Radio says no rain in sight, either."

"Harlan's worried about the cattle," Nancy explained on the way to the house. "Besides these in the pasture here, he has almost a hundred and fifty in pastures at the back of the farm. He made three trips to Nashville last September and bought them on the open market. Daddy's awfully proud of him because he picked such good stock. They came through the winter fine, and Harlan hopes to have them in prime condition to sell this fall. He paid twenty-five thousand dollars for them, but of course he had to borrow most of the money. If everything goes well, he can sell them for forty-five thousand."

"Seems to me he's taking the hard way to get rich quick."

"It's a farmer's way to make a profit honestly. And Harlan's smart enough, and he works hard enough to do it if everything were in his favor. But everything depends on the pastures, and if it doesn't rain soon—"

"It always has rained, hasn't it?" asked Monica. "Sooner or later?"

As soon as breakfast was over and the dishes were washed, Monica announced that she must write letters. She brought her stationery and pen from the bedroom and made herself comfortable in the swing on the Kinfolks Porch overlooking Nancy's garden.

The garden was a neatly patterned place. The rows of corn and beans, okra and peppers, limas and tomatoes and cabbages, Irish potatoes and sweet potatoes were straight as rulers, and even the vines of the cucumbers and squashes seemed to mind where they were going and to trail in an orderly pattern.

While Monica was writing, she saw Nancy enter the garden with a hoe. But there was no need for the hoe. Not a Jimson weed nor clump of crab grass was anywhere to be found, and the baked earth was clodded like big marbles about the roots of the plants. Monica watched Nancy at the bottom of the garden run a heat-curled blade of corn through her fingers, and, at the upper end, next the yard fence, stoop to examine a blossoming bean plant. Pale lavender blooms sprinkled to the ground as Nancy lifted the leaves.

In the field across the driveway from the house, Monica could hear the sound of tractors as Corky and one of the hired men plowed the young corn. The dust stirred up by the plows floated over the field, coating the blades of the corn and settling on the leaves of Great-great-grandfather Fifer's silver maples.

In the machinery shed, Harlan was repairing a hay baler. The early hay crop wasn't going to amount to much, he had reported to Uncle Steve. Looked like all the lespedeza in the county was killed. Lespedeza fields were bare as a bleached bone. But rains would surely give the timothy and clover a new lease on life before the next cutting, he had prophesied hopefully.

On Bridget's Porch on the other side of the house, Doak and Benny were helping Aunt Willa with the laundry. They pumped water from the cistern to fill her tubs, switched the current on and off, and between them carried basket after basket of clothes to the clothesline for her. Monica glanced at the clothes Aunt Willa was hanging in the sun—sheets and sheets and sheets, pillow cases and towels and T-shirts and heavy blue work shirts and blue jeans, including her own jeans that had been stained with milk.

Resolutely she bent to the stationery lying on her lap. She had promised to write Mimi often.

When finally Aunt Willa started dinner, Monica sealed her letters and went to the kitchen. She didn't mind helping Aunt Willa. It was one thing to be invited by Aunt Willa to fetch jam from the fruit cellar, pour the milk, and mash the potatoes, and quite another to traipse to the barn twice every day, on Nancy's schedule, rain or shine, to milk unfriendly cows.

"What a lot of ironing there is to do in the Fifer house, Aunt Willa!" she commented as she sat on the kitchen stool between odd jobs, watching Aunt Willa roll out a pie crust. "So many sheets!"

"Have you forgotten?" said Aunt Willa. "We don't iron the sheets. A hot iron burns the fresh sweet smell of wind and sunshine out of them. We let the wind iron the sheets and the towels. Unfortunately," she added, "the wind doesn't iron anything else. Maybe you'd like to iron your clothes yourself this afternoon."

"I didn't have anything but my blue jeans," said Monica.

"That's right," agreed Aunt Willa. "So you won't have much to iron."

After lunch, as Aunt Willa sprinkled clothes, Monica plugged the iron into the socket on Bridget's Porch, spread her blue jeans on the ironing board, swished across them hastily with the iron, and threw them over the back of a chair.

"Let's get a few more of the wrinkles out," suggested Aunt Willa.

"But, Aunt Willa, they're just blue jeans. I won't wear them any place but here."

"I'll show you how." Aunt Willa ignored Monica's remark as she spread the blue jeans on the ironing board again and began painstakingly and deftly to iron a leg. "That way, Monica," she said. "You try it now."

Monica tried, half-heartedly. "But, honestly, Aunt Willa," she asked, "why must blue jeans be ironed so—so slick?"

"Monica, dear," Aunt Willa answered, "it has been a tradition in the Fifer house for a hundred years that, when you iron, you iron well. I don't believe we want to disturb that tradition, do we, you and I?"

"But, Aunt Willa, do we have to cling to the past always?" pleaded Monica. "Sometimes I think the place for tradition is out the window. Just what is the sense now in ironing blue jeans as slick as a mirror?"

Aunt Willa was thoughtful for a moment. "Did you like the apple pie we had for dinner?"

"Um-m-m!" Monica smacked her lips.

"I made the best pie I could possibly make," said Aunt Willa. "If it makes sense to make the best possible apple pie, doesn't it make sense to iron your blue jeans carefully?"

"Well, if you put it that way—yes. But I still don't see any practical sense in dolling up blue jeans this way. It just satisfies a notion. That's all."

"Don't you think it a good notion, to do well anything you're doing?"

"In most things," agreed Monica reluctantly. "But I still think you could skimp over blue jeans."

She did not skimp over them, however. Painstakingly she ironed and creased, even though Aunt Willa had turned her back and was apparently paying no attention. It was only when Monica had finished that Aunt Willa turned and casually inspected her work.

"You've done a good job," she declared. "You can be proud of it."

Monica glanced at the clothes basket heaped high with sprinkled clothes, and skirted the thought that she ought to help Aunt Willa with the rest of the ironing. They were not her clothes, she argued. And the afternoon was so very hot! And men's work trousers were such a nuisance to iron.

"Finished?" asked Aunt Willa. "I'll take over now."

Monica was glad to escape to the Kinfolks Porch. With the afternoon sun beating on it, however, it was no place to relax or to read. She wondered vaguely where Nancy was, and what she was doing. Charting, maybe.

"Where are Doak and Benny?" she called to Aunt Willa.

"They're taking lemonade to the menfolks," answered Aunt Willa.

Monica looked out over the fields. The sunbaked hills seemed to hold in the hollow of their rolling shapes a continuing, unvarying pattern of mingled sound—the racing clack-clack-clack of the tractors, the shrill, piercing rasp of cicadas, and the occasional bawling of the cattle.

"Aunt Willa?" called Monica.

"Yes?"

"I think I'll go for a ride on Firefly."

"Fine!" said Aunt Willa. "That will seem like old times to you."

In the barnyard Monica caught Firefly and saddled her, as she and Nancy had learned to do long ago.

It was truly like old times, she thought, as she turned the mare up Leary's Hill under the arch of honey-locust trees. But it was not the old times Monica was remembering as the mare jogged along. Rather, she was thinking that here was one way she could get away from everything during the summer. She could mount Firefly and ride off, with only herself and her own thoughts for company.

Up the long hill plodded Firefly, along the road that was like a deep ravine, with a high embankment on each side. But the road wasn't the same, Monica noticed. In earlier summers, the low branches of the locusts growing on the embankments had fashioned a cooling green wall that cast an eerie hue on the road. Now, light glared through, and hot wind blew down the ravine.

Monica checked Firefly and looked at the locust trees. Harlan's cattle, lined up along the fence, were stretching their necks to reach the leaves in the upper branches. Already they had stripped the lower branches. Occasionally they broke into an anguished bawling that drowned out the piercing, hot-weather chorus of the cicadas.

With a feeling of uneasiness, Monica dug her heels into Firefly's ribs and rode to the top of the hill. In earlier summers, the top had been a favorite destination. There she and Nancy, sitting on the mare, could see far and wide. The same wide view over the neighboring farms struck Monica now as being strange and ominous. The broad valley was crisscrossed, as always, with fence rows where honeysuckle and trumpet vine grew, and in the wheat fields the ripening grain swayed and billowed in the wind. But the fields of corn were a sickly green, and the hillside pastures were burned bare. Only the hollows were still green, but there the cattle had cropped the grass close to the ground. Now they stood in the shade of trees whose lower branches they had stripped of leaves, and bawled their protestations to the hilltops.

That evening after the family had listened to Uncle Steve read from the Bible, the girls climbed the stairs to bed. Nancy undressed at once and fell into bed, but Monica took her time, lingering long over hanging up her clothes, brushing her hair, putting on her nightgown.

"What are you doing?" asked Nancy with a yawn as Monica stood with the dresser drawer open, studying a small card calendar she had taken from her purse.

"Nothing much," answered Monica evasively.

After a while she turned out the light and got into bed. She lay quietly, listening to Nancy's slow breathing. Nancy could go to sleep with maddening suddenness, she thought.

Eighty more blue days, Monica said to herself, like the blue Monday just finished. Eighty more days of milking, of ironing, of being managed by Nancy and smart-alecked by

Corky. Eighty more days of listening to cattle bawl. Why didn't the Fifers do something about their hungry cattle?

She would write to her father the next morning, she decided. She would tell him what a miserable time she was having. She would stay a week longer, if that would please him, or even two weeks, to keep from hurting Aunt Willa's feelings. But eighty days of this? She couldn't stand it.

Having made her decision, Monica snuggled her head into her pillow. But the bawling of the cattle stood guard at the doorway of her senses and kept sleep from entering.

After a while she stole out of bed, and, kneeling beside the window, she folded her arms on the window sill and rested her chin on them. The velvety sky was inlaid with brilliant stars. She remembered another hot night when she and Nancy had been allowed to sleep on a quilt in the yard. They were five then. It was the first time she could remember facing a sky full of stars, and she had imagined with childish awe hearing the rush of heavenly winds through the vast, interstellar spaces. It was Aunt Willa's sky, she had thought, the wind was Aunt Willa's wind, and the stars were Aunt Willa's stars.

As she waited at the window sill, remembering, an oboe-like strain pierced the night above the bawling of the cattle; a whippoorwill from the range of hills south of the house had begun his plaintive calling. Like iridescent soap bubbles, his song was blown out extravagantly over the starlit pasture, each note rounded and full and perfect. One after another, on and on—"Whip-poor-*will*! Whip-poor-*will*! Whip-poor-*will*! Whip-poor-*will*!"

As long as the bird called, Monica knelt at the window. When finally he ceased calling, she slipped into bed again. In the dark she lay quietly, sometimes hearing the cattle bawl, sometimes not. Homesickness possessed her, a strange homesickness without a name. Remembrances of her father, of Mimi, of her gay friends and good times back at home paraded through her mind, but one by one she dismissed them. It was not for these, it was for nothing distant that she was homesick. It was for something close and intimate, deep within herself that she was craving. A thing she couldn't name. A thing she had never known existed. Some inner order. Some perfectness that could soar, strong and free, as the song of the whippoorwill had soared in the starlight from the clump of sweet-gum trees at the back of the seared hilltop pasture.

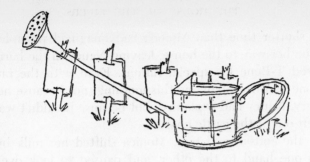

CHAPTER FOUR

Roots in the Earth

Monica opened her eyes the next morning to find Nancy up and dressing. She listened a moment. The whippoorwill— where was he now? She could hear only the hungry cattle bawling in the pasture. Drowsily she sat up in bed.

"Mornin'," Nancy greeted her cheerfully.

" 'Lo!" muttered Monica, and she flopped back on her pillow. "Seems to me I've been awake all night."

"Um-hum," said Nancy.

"Trying to fix things," said Monica. "Trying to unsnarl things. Trying to find out who I am, and what I'm doing here."

"Tell that to Corky," advised Nancy. "He likes deep subjects like that."

"I don't think I'll bother to tell Corky anything," replied Monica sourly.

Nancy laughed at her. "Going with me to milk?" she asked.

"Yes," said Monica. "If it kills me."

The milking went better this morning than before, and,

51

in a shorter time than Monica had imagined possible, she was on her way to the house, leaving Nancy in the barnyard to feed T-Bone his special rations. Even with the rations, T-Bone had been bawling this morning, not because he was hungry, Nancy had explained, but because he didn't want to be left out of the cattle chorus.

At the cottonwood tree, Monica shifted her milk bucket from one hand to the other, and paused to look over the burned fields lying at the mercy of a hot sun that was coming up still another day in a glazed sky.

"Penny for your thoughts," said Corky, coming along from the barn. "Here, let me carry the milk."

Monica let him take the bucket.

"Well," he prodded, "what were you thinking?"

"I was thinking you have to be on guard against whippoorwills," she told him.

"Monica!" he exclaimed. "I never suspected you of poetic feelings. What have the whippoorwills done to you?"

"Well, for a while last night—for just a little while—they made me think things might be different," she said. "But this morning everything's just the same."

"But you got along better with the milking," said Corky.

"I didn't like it any better, though."

"Just what do you like, Monica?"

"I don't know, Corky," she answered, grateful for his interest. "But I don't like this." She made a sweeping gesture with her arms to indicate the farm and all its activity.

"You used to like it."

"I don't any more."

"Well," he said, "why don't you go home then? You're not going to loll around here all summer to be fed, are you?"

"It wasn't my choice," she told him tartly, and marched

ahead of him into the kitchen, where the good odor of breakfast filled the air. She would write to her father the minute breakfast was finished, she decided, and tell him she wanted to go home.

As the Fifers gathered at the breakfast table, Monica, still smarting from Corky's remarks, resolved to eat only sparingly, but the sight of crisp bacon slices, scrambled eggs, and hot biscuits whetted her appetite and whittled away her resolution. As long as she was here, she decided, she might as well eat.

"Monica," said Aunt Willa, as Monica laid a thick slab of butter inside her third hot biscuit, "would you like to go to town with me this morning to take the cream?"

Monica brightened. A trip to Colgate in the midst of all the Fifer projects was quite a windfall, she thought. The letter to her father could wait. "Sure, Aunt Willa," she said. "When do we start?"

"As soon as we get the dishes washed and the house straight," said Aunt Willa.

"I can straighten up the house, Mother," Nancy offered. "There's nothing else to do." She turned to Uncle Steve. "Do you suppose it's worth while to plant a second crop of Kentucky Wonders, Daddy?" she asked. "Now's the time to plant beans if I expect to get a late crop. I was counting on them to add to my college fund," she added.

"This drought isn't doing a thing to help your college fund, is it, Nancy?" said Uncle Steve sympathetically.

"Just about one stalk of corn in ten has an ear on it," reported Nancy. "And the blossoms are falling off the beans."

"You should see my shopping list," spoke up Aunt Willa. "For the first time I can ever remember, I'm having to buy vegetables in June."

"Will you bring some bean seeds, Mother?" asked Nancy. "I can put them in the ground, and hope for rain."

"Of course, Nancy," said Aunt Willa. "Monica," she added, "would you like to plant a garden this summer, too?"

Monica let her fork drop to her plate and stared at her aunt.

"Seeds planted now won't have time to mature a crop before you go home," continued Aunt Willa. "But you can set out plants and be several weeks ahead."

It was one thing for Nancy to trap her with the milking, Monica thought, smarting under Aunt Willa's suggestion. She had rather expected Nancy to ensnare her with charts and goals and projects. But she had certainly thought better of Aunt Willa.

"What say, Monica?" sang out Corky, tauntingly.

"Corky," said Aunt Willa, "that patch of garden close to the fence that nobody had time to plant this spring—it was plowed once, but it needs spading."

"You want me to spade it," Corky stated, rather than asked.

"Would you have time?" asked Aunt Willa.

"Well," said Corky, looking at Monica, "I just want to be sure that, after it's spaded, it will be planted."

"Aunt Willa only asked you to do the spading, Corky," Monica retorted.

Half an hour later, Corky loaded a can of cream and a crate of eggs into the back of the car, and Monica climbed into the front seat to wait for Aunt Willa. She tried to recapture the luxurious feeling she had experienced when the trip was first mentioned, but the proposed garden project had scattered that to the hot winds. Still, she thought, as she watched Aunt Willa hurry down the walk to the waiting car, the trip needn't be a total waste. Aunt Willa had always understood her before. Maybe she'd be willing to listen to her now.

"What made you think I'd like to plant a garden?" she asked as Aunt Willa opened the door of the car.

With her hand on the steering wheel Aunt Willa paused and looked at her niece. "It was only a suggestion, Monica," she answered. "You don't have to plant a garden if you don't want to."

She continued to stand with her hand on the wheel as she turned her gaze from Monica to the road ahead of them. Monica remembered how she was used to fathoming the minds of the young Fifers under her roof. She wondered what Aunt Willa was thinking at that moment, what she was planning. Whatever it was didn't seem altogether diabolical, for Aunt Willa's face was so full of understanding that Monica felt almost like apologizing for her outburst.

"Do you know how to drive a car, Monica?" Aunt Willa turned once more and looked at her.

"No," Monica answered. "Daddy won't let me learn till I'm older."

"Maybe that's because New York laws are different from Kentucky laws," explained Aunt Willa. "How would you like to jump over here and drive us to the mailbox?"

"Why—do you mean, Aunt Willa—why, sure!" Monica agreed after her first faint questioning of her aunt's intentions.

She tumbled out of the car, held the door open for Aunt Willa, and then, hurrying to the other side, settled herself under the steering wheel.

"I really know how to drive," she explained. "I've watched my friend Mimi Parry, and I know just what to do."

"All you need then is a little practice," said Aunt Willa. "Let's take just a minute to give you the feel of the machinery. You know about the starter switch," she pointed as she spoke. "And the accelerator. And the clutch. And the brake pedal. Maybe you'd better practice a few starts and stops before we take off."

"Else we'd be like the man Daddy told me about who didn't know how to stop his engine and had to keep driving till he used up his gasoline," Monica said, laughing.

Suddenly she stopped. This was the first time she had laughed since she had arrived at the farm. It was a short—a very short—moment of relaxing, of forgetting herself, of enjoying life with no questions, no suspicions, no reservations, but it was long enough to change things a little, at least. She felt suddenly grateful to Aunt Willa, who had fathomed her mind better even than Monica herself could, and had come to her aid.

"Don't I have to have a permit to drive?" she asked as she started the motor.

"To drive on the highway, or on any public road," explained Aunt Willa. "But you can drive on our private lane to the mailbox without a permit. Suppose you drive down the lane a little way, and then stop. Just to be sure you know how."

"Aren't you scared, Aunt Willa?" Monica asked, laughing again. Her body tingled with the excitement she felt as the engine responded to her touch, and the car began to move.

"Oh, no," laughed Aunt Willa. "I think young people are better drivers than many older people so long as they stay within speed limits and use their heads. Now, see if you can stop."

Monica applied the brakes with sudden force, and the car
came to a jerky stop that killed the engine.

"Now, what did I do?" she exclaimed.

"You didn't put your foot on the clutch pedal," explained
Aunt Willa. "Start the motor again and try once more."

Down the lane they crept, stopping at intervals, and starting again, and laughing a great deal, until they reached the
mailbox.

"If you think you'd like to learn to drive this summer,"
said Aunt Willa as they exchanged places, "we can go to the
police station while we're in town this morning and apply
for a learner's permit. You can't get a driver's license until
you're sixteen. But with a learner's permit you can drive
anywhere you want to. The only rule is that you have to have
someone in the front seat with you who does have a driver's
license—your Uncle Steve or me, or Harlan or Coralie or
Corky."

Monica's eyes were shining. She laughed again.

"Daddy will get the shock of his life when I tell him I'm
driving a car," she said.

"That won't hurt him," declared Aunt Willa. "I think he
should have been teaching you himself."

"How long will it take to get a learner's permit?" asked
Monica.

"Oh," guessed Aunt Willa, "about a week."

She brought the car to a stop at the end of the Roller
Coaster Road, and then turned on to the highway.

"You asked me a while ago about the garden," Aunt Willa
said. "I suggested your planting one because I thought you'd
get restless and homesick staying here three months if you
didn't have some job of your own, something that depends
on you."

Monica searched her aunt's face. "You're sure you didn't suggest it because you want me to be like Nancy?" she asked.

"Heavens, no!" declared Aunt Willa. "What made you think that? I want you to be like Monica."

"You talk just like Daddy!" exploded Monica. "What am I like? That's what puzzles me."

"What they are like puzzles most fifteen-year-olds, Monica," said Aunt Willa kindly. "Fifteen is sometimes an unhappy age because boys and girls at fifteen are impatient to become themselves—sometimes so impatient that they turn into mere imitations of somebody else."

"And you think raising a garden will help me find what I'm like?" Monica asked.

"It needn't be a garden," said Aunt Willa. "It can be anything you put your heart and mind to. I suggested a garden because I thought that by raising one you could better understand us Fifers. We've always lived close to the earth, from your great-great-grandfather on down to your father, and to Nancy and Harlan and Doak. All our lives have been bound up with plowing, and planting, and fighting weeds, and waiting patiently for rain, and watching our fields burn up in times of drought, and learning to harvest with thankfulness whatever Nature has allowed us. We've found it a good life."

"I didn't know there was all that—that poetry—to farming, Aunt Willa!" exclaimed Monica. "I feel as if I've been listening to poetry."

"No fifteen-year-old knows it."

"Not even Nancy?"

"Nancy's only fifteen, like you," Aunt Willa reminded her.

Neither spoke for a moment as the car crossed the railroad tracks and rounded the slight curve in the highway.

"Nancy is counting mightily on money from T-Bone and her garden to help her through college," continued Aunt Willa. "But her garden is already ruined, I'm afraid. If something doesn't happen to T-Bone, he stands a chance to win prize money at the county fair in July, and at the state fair later. T-Bone, with blue ribbons, will give Nancy a good start toward college."

"Can't Uncle Steve send her to college?" asked Monica.

"It must all sound pretty complicated to you. You see, more people than Nancy are involved. Harlan borrowed all the ready money your Uncle Steve had to buy his cattle. Buying them was a big risk and one we cautioned him against, but, barring a drought, he had a good chance to sell them this fall at a small fortune. Harlan thinks he can wait another week for rain, but, if the drought isn't broken by then, he'll have to sell the cattle—or most of them—for whatever they'll bring. That means he's saddled with a big debt, and Harlan and Coralie are pretty young to have such a debt on their shoulders. It means Harlan can't repay what he borrowed from your Uncle Steve. And that hits Nancy a double blow, you see, because her father will have nothing for a year or two to contribute to her college fund, either."

"Gee!" said Monica. "I didn't know the drought was personal, like that. I knew it burned up the crops, and made the cattle bawl. But I—I didn't realize it did things to people, too."

"Do you like poetry?" Aunt Willa asked, abruptly changing the subject. "Have you written some, maybe, for your school paper?"

Monica turned a pleasantly surprised face toward her. "How did you know that?"

"I only suspected," said Aunt Willa. "If you'd like a garden, maybe you'd like to plant flowers instead of vegetables. I imagine you have a special flair for arranging flowers. And we could use that talent around our house."

"Aunt Willa," Monica's astonishment as she looked at her aunt was written plainly on her face, "you're telling me things I didn't know about myself. But they're true. How did you know?"

Aunt Willa smiled. "I think I'll keep that a secret. Some day you'll find out how I know. While we're in town," she continued, "we'll go to the greenhouse and see if they have any flower plants—petunias, or marigolds, or asters. These'll bloom while you're with us."

"But, Aunt Willa," objected Monica, "if Nancy's vegetables can't grow in the drought, how will flowers grow?"

"We won't get many," said Aunt Willa. "Maybe a dozen or so. You can set them out near the garden fence, and water them the first few days. Maybe by the time they take root, we'll have a rain. And when the flowers bloom, you can keep a fresh bouquet on the dining table for us."

"Sure!" agreed Monica enthusiastically. "And I guess that'll put Corky in his place."

"Is Corky out of his place?" asked Aunt Willa.

"He asked me this morning why I'm sticking around all summer if I'm not going to contribute something to the family," Monica told her.

"Corky believes in free speech, doesn't he?" Aunt Willa smiled. "Well, before the summer's over, I expect you to make him eat those careless words."

They had reached Colgate now and were driving down

a sultry street lined with ash trees from which yellowed leaves peppered the sidewalk. In a yard, children in bathing trunks played noisily in the spray of a lawn sprinkler. It seemed even hotter and drier in town than in the country.

"We were talking about how fifteen-year-olds find themselves," Aunt Willa said. "There's just one rule you need to follow, and that's a very simple one. Do the common jobs that come your way uncommonly well. That'll bring out the real Monica almost before you know it. Now, let's get rid of the cream and the eggs, and then go for the permit and some flower plants."

To Monica the morning seemed in a special way to be her morning. She felt a tingle of excitement as she filled out the application at the police station for her learner's permit. At the florist's, Aunt Willa allowed her to pick and choose as she fancied, from the meager offerings.

"White and gold and bronze," she mused when the florist identified his tight-budded zinnias. "A big bunch of white and bronze zinnias in a bowl—wouldn't that be a study for van Gogh, Aunt Willa!" she exclaimed.

But the best part of the morning was when Aunt Willa exchanged places with her at the mailbox on their way home, and allowed her to drive over the private lane to the house.

"Whew!" exclaimed Monica as she brought the car to a jerky stop at the front gate. "I did it, Aunt Willa!"

"When the car isn't in use and you aren't busy with something else, Monica," Aunt Willa said as they climbed out, "you may practice driving. It helps to practice starting and stopping and backing till you can do them without thinking of all the details. And when you want to drive to the mailbox and back, one of us will be glad to go with you. Your uncle would enjoy nothing better, I'm sure." They joined Uncle Steve under the maples.

"So your Aunt Willa has a new chauffeur!" he exclaimed. "Tell me about it, Monica."

Monica plunged at once into a recital of her morning's experiences, describing in detail how it felt to drive the car, and laughing at her mistakes.

"Know what you ought to do?" suggested Uncle Steve. "Get a couple of old orange crates out of the kindling bin, and set them up for parked cars out here at the gate. Then practice parking between them. What's that in your hand?"

"My garden," Monica told him. "Zinnia plants I'm going to set out. Going to keep the Fifer table supplied with centerpieces."

"Corky's got your ground spaded," Uncle Steve told her. "But as one gardener to another, I'd advise you to dampen the roots of your zinnias and keep the plants in the fruit cellar where it's cool. Wait till the sun goes down to set them out."

At the lunch table, Nancy reminded the Fifers that the county 4-H style show was to be held in the Colgate High school gym that afternoon.

"What do you do at that? What stores furnish the clothes?" asked Monica, thinking of style shows at home.

"Stores!" laughed Nancy. "We model our own clothes, the ones we've made. I'm going to model a square-dance dress I made."

"Oh," said Monica flatly.

"That leaves you out, eh, Monica?" said Corky.

"It doesn't leave her out," said Nancy scoldingly. "She'll enjoy meeting the girls and seeing the clothes they've made."

"I really had planned to do something else," said Monica.

"I need the car to take your Uncle Steve to the doctor, Monica." Aunt Willa sensed Monica's intentions. "I think you'll find it interesting to see the clothes the girls have made, and to meet the girls. I can drive you and Nancy in when we go to the doctor, and somebody can come for you."

Having her pleasant plans for the afternoon changed so abruptly was to Monica like having someone sitting opposite her on a seesaw jump off and leave her to hit the ground hard. But with Corky eying her, she could think of no reasons for refusing to go with Nancy.

The style show was as dull as Monica had suspected it would be. Fifty girls, big and little, were there, she estimated, and a half-grown boy, all ignoring her while they watched an officious woman, full of talk and directions and orders, examine every garment from neckline to hem bottom, and inside out, and front to back. There were also a dozen or more proud mamas, sitting in the chairs arranged in stiff rows in the gym. Monica wondered what the lone boy was doing there.

Two hours—two long, hot, close, depressing hours—passed before ribbons were finally pinned on the few fortunate dresses, Nancy's among them. The girls were called, a group at a time, to model their dresses. For almost another hour Monica sat wilted and dejected back of the mamas and watched girls parade self-consciously across the front row of the bleachers. Out of the entire group, only Nancy and two or three others, she thought, exhibited their dresses with the swish and the flair of a real model. And Nancy, she admitted, petite and dark and sparkling, did look darling in her wide, flaring skirt, and off-the-shoulder blouse.

Near the end of the show, the officious judge with the boy

in tow came hurrying to Monica in the back of the room.

"Honey," said the woman in a loud whisper, "Mike wants to ask a favor of you. Since you're not modeling a dress of your own, he thought maybe you'd model his garment for him."

Monica stared at the tow-headed, blue-jeaned, grinning boy.

"You mean—you made a dress?"

"Uh-uh," said the boy. "Apron."

"What for?" she asked.

"For my mother," he said.

"His mother couldn't come," explained the woman, "and he wants a model. Could you—would you?"

Monica wanted to resist. Here she was, trapped again into something she didn't want to do.

"It'll just fit you," the boy said, grinning confidently.

"Come with me to the dressing room," said the woman, and before Monica could find a way to refuse, she was walking across the gymnasium at her heels, trailed by the unabashed boy.

At least, thought Monica on the way, modeling an apron was preferable to pinning down a hot chair any longer. She hoped the garment would be frilly and dainty, on the order of Nancy's dress.

"You wait here, Mike," the woman said to the boy at the door of the dressing room. "She'll come out and show you when she gets the apron on."

Inside the dressing room, Monica's spirits fell with a thud when the woman handed her the apron. Made of a feed sack, it was as plain as an apron can be—full length, straight, with a neck strap of bias tape and two slim strings for tying in the back.

"You look just fine!" declared the woman as Monica put the apron on. "Just step outside the door there and let Mike see."

Grimly, Monica obeyed.

"Gee, you look swell!" declared Mike.

"Well, say," quipped Monica sarcastically, "I've got to know you better. You're so original in your occupation and your taste."

A recollection stirred in her mind—do the common jobs that come your way uncommonly well. That was Aunt Willa's recipe, given her only that morning.

Back in the dressing room, Monica paused to look at her reflection in the mirror before walking out to the bleachers. She might have been a feed sack herself, she thought—a long, stringy feed sack, since the apron almost touched her feet.

"Ready?" asked the women. "Let's hurry and get this over with."

"Just a second," said Monica, wishing some fairy god-mother would suddenly appear and change the feed sack apron into a sparkling evening gown. Once more she looked into the mirror. Then, pushing her upswept hair becomingly into place, she lifted her head high, walked with a sophisti-cated saunter from the dressing room to the center of the bleachers, paused briefly, and began turning around slowly as she had been instructed to do.

Applause broke out, especially loud in the back of the room.

Monica glanced hastily in the direction of the loud ap-plause. There, just inside the door, stood Corky. For a second she froze. Why, she asked herself, if he had to come for her and Nancy—why did he have to pick that humiliating mo-ment to arrive?

Momentarily, she glared at him. Then, as she resumed turning, she caught sight of a big, bright smile on Mike's face. The smile brought to mind once more Aunt Willa's instructions to do the common things uncommonly well. Resolutely, she turned, not twice as the woman had told her to do, but three times for the group to see and to admire Mike's handiwork. Then, to the sound of further applause, she sauntered regally off the bleachers, with the feed sack apron flapping about her ankles.

"Don't you wish you were smart enough, Corky Fifer, to make your mother an apron like that?" she said loftily, as she and Nancy climbed into the car.

"When I do make one," teased Corky, "I know whom I'll ask to model it."

"It isn't a foregone conclusion that her answer will be yes," she retorted.

The sun was almost down when they reached home. As soon as Monica had changed to blue jeans, she went to the garden to set out her zinnias. Uncle Steve rolled his wheel chair to the fence where he could give her directions for digging holes, for firming the earth about the roots of the plants, for watering them, and for mulching the topsoil to keep the moisture in the ground as long as possible.

"What you doing, Monicky?" called Benny curiously as he and Doak came from the corncrib with feed for the hens.

"Planting my own garden," said Monica. "Want to help?"

"Sure!" said Benny.

"We'll pump water and carry it for you," offered Doak.

The boys not only brought water. They separated the plants and handed them to Monica as she dug holes in the clods, they poured water gently about the roots of each plant, and they watched the dark watered spots deepen and spread.

As they worked, they made small, intimate conversation with Monica that, set in the vast, raucous desert of sound made by the cattle and the cicadas, was like a friendly, green oasis.

And the roots of her own plants, about which she was firming the earth, were another oasis, she sensed—the least reliable kind of oasis, to be sure, but still an oasis—ringed by a long, hot summer, jobs she disliked, and hours to be spent with Nancy, who would like to understand her but couldn't, and Corky, who could understand her but wouldn't.

Maybe Aunt Willa was wise in suggesting the garden. Like bad-tasting medicine, Aunt Willa's advice was hard to take. But, having taken it, already she was beginning to feel better.

"Aunt Willa's got lots of eggs tonight," announced Benny as he stared at the heaped-up egg basket his aunt was carrying from the hen house.

Around the last plant Monica gently raked dry earth over the wet ground to hold in the moisture.

"Aunt Willa's all right, isn't she, Benny?" she said.

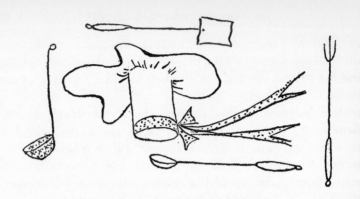

CHAPTER FIVE

Hay While the Sun Shines

Harlan dropped by at the hour of bedtime the next evening, carrying in his hand a few stalks of timothy and clover he had plucked from the hayfield.

"Feel these, Dad," he said to Uncle Steve.

Uncle Steve took the stalks and studied them.

Monica looked at Harlan, remembering all that Aunt Willa had told her about his purchase of the cattle. It wasn't the mere passing of time, she sensed, that made him seem quieter, more thoughtful, and years older than the Harlan she remembered from earlier summers. It was Uncle Steve's illness that had tested him, and all kinds of weather that had kept him continually on trial, demanding that he make up his mind whether to plant corn one day or the next, whether to sow wheat now or later, whether to mow the hay tomorrow or next week.

Monica recalled haymaking on the Fifer farm in earlier summers. Then Uncle Steve had kept one eye on the ripening timothy and clover and the lespedeza, and the other on the heavens for signs of rain. On the day appointed for haying to begin, Harlan, as sure as the gayest lark in the meadow that all was right with the world, had mounted the tractor as soon as the dew was off the grass, and started jauntily on his long trips around the hayfield. He had left in the wake of the mowing machine wide, ribboned swaths of hay, curing in the sun. Haying had seemed to get into the men's blood, like a fever, she remembered, and nothing gave them rest until the hay was properly cured to its aromatic tea-green stage, and the baler had neatly packaged and tied it and tossed it off to be hauled to the barn and stored in the loft.

Nearly always, too, Monica remembered, there had been complications, just as complications might develop to aggravate an illness. In the middle of the haying, corn reached the cultivation stage, or the wheat ripened, or the mowing machine broke down, or the heavens opened and torrents of rain fell on the new-mown hay, making it difficult to cure, and questionable to store in the barn. But never were there such complications as the drought was forcing on Harlan now.

Uncle Steve twisted the stalks of timothy and clover in his hands.

"I believe it's ready, Harlan," he said.

"With the wind this hot and dry," said Harlan, "we won't even need to cure the hay. We can bale it as we cut it."

"Your machinery all ready?"

"Yes," answered Harlan. "Corky can run the mower. Cowboy Mullins can rake, and I'll run the baler. There won't be any dew, so we can get in the fields before sunup. It oughtn't take us more than five days."

"Just the timothy and clover?" asked Uncle Steve, thoughtfully studying the stalks lying in the palm of his hand.

"That's all. And only half a crop of that," Harlan told him. "No lespedeza at all. In the whole lespedeza field, Dad, there isn't a green leaf." He turned to Corky. "You ready for the big push? Before sunup?"

"Sure thing," answered Corky, as cocksure as Harlan had been in the earlier summers, when the decisions were Uncle Steve's to make.

"Doak," asked Aunt Willa, "you and Benny ready for bed? It'll keep you humping tomorrow to carry ice water and lemonade to these haymakers."

"We're just waiting," answered Doak as he glanced significantly at the Bible that lay unopened on the table.

A stir passed through the Fifers as if, a decision having been made, they were free to get on with their usual bedtime occupations. Harlan, however, made no move to go, but continued standing in the doorway.

He looked tired, Monica thought, on the eve of haymaking, when he should have looked strong and toughened, and cocksure, like Corky. Walking hourly with the hard, unrelenting drought had made him tight-lipped and grim-faced, and the hot, searing air seemed to have dried up the springs of his drive and energy, as they were drying up the pastures.

"John Jarvis sold his cattle today, Dad," he said.

The mention of cattle seemed to bring the raucous bawling of the Fifer herd into the living room in a fresh gust of sound.

"He did? What did he get for them?" asked Uncle Steve, thoughtfully.

"Twenty-three cents," said Harlan. "Bought 'em in September for thirty cents, and some of 'em weighed less when he sold them than when he bought them."

"His pasture all gone?"

"Pasture dried up, and ponds, too," explained Harlan.

"What about our ponds?" asked Uncle Steve.

"You remember, I told you our pond at the far end of the west pasture's gone."

"The bottom of that pond's crisscrossed with cracks half a foot deep," reported Corky. "Looks like a big prehistoric tortoise shell."

"The two on the east side of the farm'll be gone by the end of this week," said Harlan.

Uncle Steve sat watching Harlan with a yearning in his face.

"Sit down, son," he said.

He reached for the Bible, and thumbed through its thin leaves as Harlan dropped into a chair beside Aunt Willa.

Then shalt thou call, and the Lord shall answer;
thou shalt cry, and he shall say, Here I am.

Quiet possessed them all as they sat listening to Uncle Steve's calm, rich voice reading words so steadfast and so enduring that they drowned out the wearisome bawling of the cattle, and tempered the dry, hot wind.

If thou take away from the midst of thee the yoke,
the putting forth of the finger,
and speaking vanity;
and if thou draw out thy soul to the hungry,
and satisfy the afflicted soul;
then shall thy light rise in obscurity,

and thy darkness be as the noon day;
and the Lord shall guide thee continually,
and satisfy thy soul in drought,
and make fat thy bones;
and thou shalt be like a watered garden,
and like a spring of water, whose waters fail not.
And they that shall be of thee shall build the old waste
   places:
thou shalt raise up the foundations of many generations;
and thou shalt be called,
The repairer of the breach,
The restorer of paths to dwell in.

In the quiet that followed Uncle Steve's reading, Harlan got to his feet.

"Good night, Dad," he said, affectionately. "Good night, Mother."

He kissed Aunt Willa on the cheek, and went out the door, across the Kinfolks Porch, out into the starry night, newly clad, it seemed, in some invisible but durable armor against the drought and all its ruin.

"Why does it make so much difference if the haylofts aren't bursting with hay?" Monica asked Nancy when they were lying in bed. Her mind was full of puzzles. "Even if Harlan keeps the cattle, they'd be sold before winter, wouldn't they?"

"Yes, in September or October," Nancy explained. "But by that time Harlan should have a new herd ready to fatten for next fall. And during the winter the cattle need hay."

Monica lay silent.

"If it rains soon, he'll have a small crop of hay from the timothy and clover fields he's going to begin cutting tomorrow," explained Nancy. "But the lespedeza is killed already, roots and all. The new seedings Harlan planted in the spring have died, too. And even if he planted more seeds now, they wouldn't come up. That means he can't feed many cattle next year, either."

Long afterward Monica listened to Nancy turning fitfully in bed and fanning her hot face with her hands. She remembered that Aunt Willa had suggested she plant a garden and tend it through the drought so that she might better understand the Fifers. But how was she to understand fully the troubles that were keeping Nancy awake and thrashing about in the dark when she herself had sacrificed nothing to the drought? Even if the sun baked her zinnias as it had baked Nancy's beans, the drought was doing her no real harm. She was uncomfortable enough, to be sure, in a room that felt like a furnace. But in the late summer her discomfort was coming to an end, and she was going home where no drought had visited, back to her father, and an orderly housekeeper who asked no questions, and Mimi.

Mimi? The probing shaft of thought sank to a deeper level. What had happened to Mimi? Mimi seemed only half real, like a character out of a piece of popular fiction.

Early the next morning, the rising sun blazed down from a glazed, sick-looking sky onto feverish activity in the hayfield where Corky mowed the hay, Cowboy Mullins raked it into windrows, and Harlan baled it. Before the hour when ordinarily the dew was off the grass, ragged rows of bales were lengthening from fence row to the center of the field where Harlan was tossing bales off the machine to be picked up by the truck.

Above the clatter made by the breakfast dishes as she and Uncle Steve washed and dried them, Monica was conscious of the noises outdoors—the metallic clack-clack-clack of the mowing machine, the bawling of the cattle along the pasture fence rows, the screeching of the cicadas in the heat. Combined, they were full of discord, like modern music, she thought. But the theme was plainly one of tragedy. Not the least understanding of persons could fail to feel that. She wondered what a girl with no personal stake in the tragedy might do about it, other than loll around all summer to be fed, as Corky had bluntly suggested.

Monica, drying the last of the silver, walked to the door and watched Aunt Willa sprinkling clothes on Bridget's Porch.

"Want me to iron some this morning?" she asked.

"If you want to," agreed Aunt Willa. "I thought, though, while the car isn't being used this morning, you might like to practice your driving."

"I'll iron my clothes first," said Monica. "Mine and Benny's."

"Nancy has a book on driving that will help you," Aunt Willa told her. "I'll ask her to find it for you."

The morning was half gone when finally Monica, with Nancy's book in her hand, settled herself under the steering wheel of the car that was parked in front of the house, and set to work. The rest of the week, during the haying, she spent hours at a time, morning and afternoon, studying the book, starting and stopping and backing the car, parking between orange crates, raising the hood and identifying the parts of the engine, and, several times a day, with Aunt Willa or Uncle Steve beside her, driving over the private lane to the mailbox and back again.

"Your learner's permit ought to be here any day now," said Aunt Willa as she rode with Monica to the mailbox on Mon-

day afternoon. "When it comes, you may drive any place—
on the highway, in town, anywhere we go—so long as you
drive safely. You've learned your driving lessons well, Monica."

"Thanks, Aunt Willa," said Monica.

Aunt Willa puckered her brow a moment in thought. "I'll
tell you what let's do," she suggested. "Nancy has an all-day
county 4-H meeting in Morganfield tomorrow, and I want
to attend a meeting on chickens that's scheduled for ten in
the morning. And your Uncle Steve has an appointment with
the doctor. You let me take the wheel and we'll drive to the
post office. If your permit should by any chance be there—
and I have a hunch it may—we can get it this afternoon and
not have to wait for the postman to deliver it tomorrow.
Then you can drive us to Morganfield."

"Aunt Willa! Do you mean that?"

"Why not? Wouldn't you like to?"

"Of course. Drive to Morganfield? I'd like nothing better."

Aunt Willa's hunch was correct. They found the permit in
the post office.

"We'll scotch tape it right into the glove compartment
beside Nancy's so you'll always have it when you're driving,"
said Aunt Willa. "And you can get your first experience in
highway driving by taking us home."

Taping the small instrument of the law to the door of the
glove compartment gave Monica a feeling of importance.
But when she took the wheel of the car and drove safely
through the Colgate Main Street traffic and out on the highway, she felt such a satisfaction as she could never remember
having had before. Occasionally a car overtook her on the
highway, or she had to pass a slow-moving piece of farm

machinery. Each such experience loomed in the rear-view mirror or ahead as a small crisis. Gradually, however, her confidence grew, and by the time she drove up to the Fifer gate she was relaxed, and completely happy.

The next morning at breakfast, Uncle Steve sat watching Corky. "Think you can hold out?" he asked.

"Me?" scoffed Corky. "I'm going fine. And since today's our last day," he looked meaningfully at Aunt Willa, "I'll be thinking all morning about the larrupin' dinner that'll be waiting for us."

It was Aunt Willa's turn to look at Corky.

"We womenfolks are going to walk out on you today, Corky," she said. "We're leaving you to batch, you and Doak and Benny."

"To batch!" groaned Corky. "Where are you going?"

"We have to go to Morganfield," Aunt Willa told him.

"Why can't you go to Morganfield tomorrow?" he asked.

"The meetings are today, Corky," explained Aunt Willa. "And your Uncle Steve's appointment with the doctor is today, too."

Monica looked at Corky, and for the first time she saw him not as a cocksure young-man-about-to-enter-college but as a tired boy—a boy to whom the drought had become personal, too. Under the gruelling haymaking, he had grown lean, and hollow-eyed from weariness, and when he moved it was as if all his muscles groaned in protest.

"I know," spoke up Benny. "We can eat dinner with Coralie."

"Coralie hasn't been feeling well, Benny," explained Aunt Willa. "You can get along all right for one meal. Doak, there are a few early apples in the orchard. You and Benny go for them right after breakfast. I'll make an extra deep apple pie for your lunch before I go. And tonight, when we're home and you're through with the hay, Corky, we'll celebrate with the best meal I can scrape together. The vegetable bins in the stores aren't too full, but there'll be plenty of fried chicken, and supper will be special, I promise."

"How about our lemonade?" Corky asked. "What happens to that if you go away?"

"I'll make it before I go," promised Aunt Willa. "Leave it in the refrigerator. Doak and Benny can get it out and carry it to you. Can't you, boys?"

"Yes'm," they promised.

Things happened that morning, however, that were not on Aunt Willa's schedule. She had no sooner rolled Uncle Steve's chair down the steps so that he could wait for them in the shade of the maples than the telephone began to ring. "What do you do for roupy chickens?" one neighbor telephoned, and Aunt Willa, who was the community's recognized authority on chickens, had to go into detail about treating hens that have fallen into a sickly decline. Another neighbor called to pass the time of day.

"Couldn't she have waited till tonight to talk about the weather?" asked Nancy impatiently as Aunt Willa finally hung up the receiver and hurried to the kitchen. "After all, it's here to stay, it seems."

"She's listened to her cattle too long," said Aunt Willa, sympathetically. "She wanted somebody to perk her spirits up." She glanced anxiously at the clock. "Wonder where those boys are with the apples?"

"I can peel the apples for you," offered Monica, anxious to be off and driving the car.

"We'll have to have them first," said Aunt Willa. She stood a minute in the doorway, looking off where the apple orchard with its row of beehives along the edge fanned out on the hill. Seeing no sign of Doak and Benny, she started in search of them.

She found the boys sitting on the fence back of the barn, discussing fantail pigeons, and with not an apple gathered.

"Boys," Aunt Willa's voice was unusually stern, "why haven't you gathered the apples?"

At that moment a lamb, caught by its foot in the wire fence on one side of its yard, began a sorrowful bleating that saved Doak and Benny from Aunt Willa's scolding. They ran to free it. Its leg was cut, and ten valuable minutes passed before Aunt Willa could find the salve which Benny had borrowed to put on a kitten's leg and had not returned to its proper place. And after that the apples had to be gathered.

"Girls," said Aunt Willa despairingly as she set the basket of apples on the sink and glanced at the kitchen clock, "what'll we do? We have to leave right away if I'm to get to that meeting on time. The lemonade isn't made. The pie's not baked. There isn't time even to peel the apples, Monica."

"Couldn't Corky eat leftovers just once?" Nancy asked. She was furiously polishing shoes on Bridget's Porch.

"And drink water instead of lemonade?" asked Monica.

"Of course, it isn't as if he had to eat leftovers all the time," argued Nancy.

"Leftovers once would make him appreciate what he gets every day," declared Monica.

As she spoke, Monica remembered Corky's lean, brown face, his tired eyes, the way he half-dragged, half-hurried toward the hayfield with the sun blazing down on him.

Quickly she dismissed him from her mind. Corky was tough, she told herself. He could take it, even on leftovers.

In fact, it served him right for talking like a Dutch uncle to her.

She glanced at Aunt Willa who, with hands pressed on the kitchen sink, was staring first at the clock, then at the apples. It wasn't like Aunt Willa, she thought, to be so torn between decisions. And, she had to admit, it wasn't like Aunt Willa to walk out on the menfolks, even if she and Nancy did.

She went slowly upstairs and began dressing. But she wasn't thinking of dressing, nor even of driving the car to Morganfield. She was seeing Aunt Willa trying to make up her mind to leave a hard-working boy to a dinner of cold leftovers.

For minutes, Monica tried to dismiss Aunt Willa's concern. There was no sense in her babying Corky. He didn't need it, and he didn't deserve it. But hadn't Aunt Willa babied her a little, too? Maybe, the idea popped into her mind, Aunt Willa knew when a homesick Fifer needed a little babying.

At last, thoughtfully, and not without self-pity, Monica pulled her dress back over her head, put it on a hanger, and hung it in the closet. She put on her blue jeans and went slowly down to the kitchen.

"I don't have to go, Aunt Willa," she announced. "I'll stay home and get dinner."

"Oh, no, Monica!" Nancy protested.

"But you'd counted so on going," said Aunt Willa. "It's like cheating you to leave you home. I'd not go myself, but. . . ."

Monica thought of the prized Plymouth Rocks strutting about the chicken lots. They were the result, she knew, not of chance, but of study and work on Aunt Willa's part, and of things she'd learned attending meetings such as this one.

"Honestly, I don't mind," Monica said. Anyway, she argued to herself, if she went she might be assigned the ignominious honor of modeling another apron at one of Nancy's meetings. "There'll be lots of days I can drive the car," she added.

"Bless you, Monica!" Aunt Willa declared warmly. "Can you bake an apple pie?"

"No," said Monica. "But I can make the lemonade. And maybe, if I had a recipe, I could make some cookies for dinner. And tell me what's for dinner. I'll do the best I can."

"Monica, child . . ." Aunt Willa began, but she seemed unable to finish what she had started to say. Reaching for a pencil and paper, she hastily wrote down a menu, took a package of meat from the freezer, told Monica where to find the other items on the menu, pointed out a particular cookbook, and rushed off to dress.

Fifteen minutes later as Aunt Willa, Nancy, and Uncle Steve drove away down the lane, Monica waved good-by from the Sociable Porch, and turned dutifully back to the kitchen. She and Nancy had washed the dishes, but they hadn't washed the cream separator. If Aunt Willa was a stickler for anything, it was that a separator should not be allowed to stand with milk drying on its parts. She'd better begin by washing it, she decided.

She prepared a hot, soapy water in the dishpan, put water on to boil in the teakettle, and confronted the separator.

"People are too clever at hiding things," she muttered, looking for a screw, a bolt, or a knob that would release the bowl.

She tried to remove the milk and cream spouts, but without success. Somewhere inside the separator, she knew, were metal disks—dozens of them in a tight row—that Aunt Willa ran onto a rod, shook out for dear life, and washed, scalded, and dried in the wink of an eye. But the whereabouts of the disks was a mystery.

When continued searching revealed nothing, Monica grasped the edge of the bowl in both hands and gave a mighty wrench. Off spun the bowl into her arms. Recovered from this surprise, she found that a slight turn released the spouts. Even the disks were no great trouble to remove, once she found the rod Aunt Willa used for washing them.

What required Aunt Willa ten minutes to do, Monica did in half an hour, and not expertly, either. The disks presented the biggest problem. Aunt Willa could flick them apart and dry them, one after the other, like a clock ticking seconds away, but, in Monica's inexperienced hands, they clung together and moved awkwardly on the rod.

At last, however, they were washed, scalded, and dried, and Monica was about to fit them into the separator again when suddenly they slipped off the rod, and with a dismal clattering and clanging, went wheeling in every direction across the kitchen floor. At that moment she heard the stamp of hurrying feet on the Kinfolks Porch, and Doak jerked open the screen door, and burst into the kitchen, his face white, his eyes bulging with fright.

"They're after us, Monica!" he yelled. "Help! Help!"

"What in the world is this?" demanded Monica.

Without pausing to answer, Doak charged across the disk-cluttered kitchen, across Bridget's Porch, and out into the back yard.

From the Kinfolks Porch came the sound of Benny's frightened voice.

"Monicky! Monicky! They've got us!"

As he flung open the screen door, Benny tripped and fell headlong into the kitchen, and with him came a dozen angry honey bees, buzzing and diving about his head.

"Ow! Ow!" yelled Benny. "He stung me, Monicky!"

"Doak!" shrieked Monica, sending disks clattering as she ducked under the table for refuge. "Come back here! Come and get these things out!"

"Ow! It hurts!" sobbed Benny, and, scrambling to his feet, he dashed across the kitchen and through the doorway after Doak, leaving the maddened bees darting about the room.

Cautiously leaving her refuge, Monica dodged the bees, and followed Benny out of the kitchen. She saw Doak running in the direction of the hayfield.

"Benny! Doak!" she shouted. "Come back here and help get those bees out of the kitchen!"

Benny stopped running. He turned and walked back to Monica. He was still crying.

"A bee sting doesn't hurt that much, does it?" Monica asked.

"Yes, it does, too," sobbed Benny. "I bet you never got stung by a bee."

"Where did it sting you?" she asked.

"Right here," he sobbed, gingerly touching the back of his neck.

"I'll take the stinger out," Monica offered. "Then you can put mud on the place where the bee stung you."

She removed the stinger between the nails of her thumb and forefinger.

"Why were the bees chasing you? That's what I'd like to know," she said.

Reluctantly Doak walked toward her.

"What did you do to the bees, Doak?" she asked.

"We just wanted a little honey," explained Doak sheepishly. "We lifted up the top of the hive just a little bit."

"Just a teeny weeny little bit," added Benny.

"And now you're stung, Benny, and the kitchen's full of bees," scolded Monica. "I stayed home from Morganfield to cook your dinner. But how do you expect me to get dinner with mad bees chasing me around the stove? You may have to go hungry for this," she warned.

Under the threat of hunger the boys were spurred to concentration.

"We might kill 'em with a fly swatter," Benny whimpered.

"All right," agreed Monica. "There's a fly swatter on Bridget's Porch, hanging by the door. Two swatters, in fact. You boys call me when you've got the kitchen cleared."

A grin brightened Benny's tear-streaked face. "You don't mean it, Monicky," he ventured.

"Of course Uncle Steve isn't going to like having his bees killed," she said.

"I know," Doak said, brightening. "I'll bet Corky can get 'em out."

"Then you hotfoot it to the hayfield and bring Corky," commanded Monica. "No," she said on second thought, "don't bring Corky. Bring Harlan. Or Cowboy."

The boys hurried off toward the hayfield. In a quarter hour they returned, running along at the heels of Corky, who was complaining loudly about having to leave the hay. He was so disgruntled that he didn't notice Monica, who was waiting in the front yard under the maples. He hurried into the kitchen, stationed himself in one corner of the room and Doak in another with newspapers to fan the bees toward the doorway, and ordered Benny to hold the screen door open. In a few minutes the kitchen was free of bees.

"Where's that lemonade you boys were to bring?" scolded Corky. "And what are these separator disks doing all over the floor, I'd like to know."

"How should I know?" shrugged Doak.

"I dropped them, Corky," said Monica, entering the kitchen.

"And what are you doing here?" Corky stared at her. "I thought everybody went to Morganfield."

"I decided not to go," she told him. "I stayed home to fix dinner."

"Well, for crying out loud! You didn't need to do that!" he said. "Here, Doak and Benny," he turned quickly to the boys, "help me pick up these disks."

By the time Monica had helped Benny put mud on the bee sting, made the lemonade, and started the boys on their way to the field, the clock said dinner must be on. Pork chops, Aunt Willa had written on the menu. Potatoes and carrots. And applesauce. Benny liked applesauce heated, with a pinch of cloves in it. Fix it that way. Monica marveled at Aunt Willa's knack for adding special touches to please even the least of nephews, and that a presently delinquent one, too.

Between putting the chops to frying, peeling potatoes, and scraping carrots, Monica mixed her cookie dough painstakingly according to the recipe. By eleven-thirty the cookies were cooling on racks on Bridget's Porch. At eleven-thirty, too, Doak and Benny returned from the hayfield.

"Say," Monica bargained with them. "I'll give you boys something if you'll set the table. Though you ought to do it for nothing," she added.

"How much?" bargained Doak.

Come and see," invited Monica, leading the way to Bridget's Porch, and giving each of them two cookies.

"Shucks, man!" sighed Doak, opening his eyes wide.

Benny took a cookie and bit into it. "You're a good cook, Monicky," he pronounced solemnly.

Monica glowed. To win the hearts of two small cousins with cookies of her own making was almost as good as driving to Morganfield, she told herself. And just wait. Before dinner was over, she'd win Corky, too.

Leading the way to the kitchen, she handed each of the boys some silverware. "Get going, now," she ordered. "Corky'll be here before you know it. Put Corky at one end, at Uncle Steve's place, and me at the other, at Aunt Willa's. You boys can sit at the sides."

They took the silverware into the dining room. After a few minutes, Monica glanced at the clock.

"Boys," she called, "get a move on."

Immediately they came hurrying into the kitchen by way of Bridget's Porch.

"Here are the plates," said Monica, handing Benny four plates.

"We'll carry just one plate at a time," announced Doak. "So we won't break 'em."

They were at heart very nice, responsible boys, Monica decided.

Benny trotted off with one plate, Doak with another. But it seemed to Monica they were a long time returning for the others.

"Hurry!" she called. "There's salt and pepper to put on, too. And milk. And bread and butter."

"Don't worry!" Doak consoled her as he entered the kitchen from the porch. "We'll get 'em all there."

By the time they had finished, Corky had arrived, and Monica began dishing up the dinner. The platter of pork chops, wreathed with vegetables, she put in front of Corky to serve.

With the serving fork, Corky lifted the pork chops to the plates, and he spooned out the vegetables. Aunt Willa's pork chops were always tender and juicy, her vegetables plump and tasty and steamy. Monica's pork chops were dark brown in color, and, when Corky served them, they clattered on the plates like dried chips of wood. The potatoes were soggy and the carrots were burned.

Monica felt as dejected as the dinner looked. She wondered what Corky was thinking of it. He was being gallant enough not to remark about the food, anyway. Oh, well, she had done the best she could. He'd at least have to admit the cookies were good.

Remembering her upbringing as mistress in her own house, Monica attempted to keep conversation running smoothly, but Corky seemed too tired for light conversation. He seemed almost too tired to eat. Benny, too, sat with most of his food untouched on his plate.

In the middle of the meal, Monica studied Benny. Always a slow eater, he now sat with one of his cheeks puffed out like a nut-carrying chipmunk's.

Benny noticed she was watching him. He stared a moment at his plate. Then, lifting pleading eyes in Corky's direction, he muttered around the pork chop stuffed in his cheek, "Excuse me, please."

Corky studied Benny's overstuffed cheek.

"You bet!" he said understandingly.

Monica wanted to burst into tears. Still, they had all been pretty decent not to say what they were thinking.

That marked some kind of milestone for Corky, she felt sure.

"You don't have to finish your chop," Monica said to Benny as he returned to the dining room minus the lump. "We'll have our dessert now."

Corky helped her clear the table for dessert. He was doing what he could to show his appreciation, she realized. She hoped he'd forget the main course when he had eaten the dessert.

"I'll take the applesauce in," she said to him in the kitchen when they had finished clearing the table. "You bring what's on the porch. Here's a plate."

As she set the dish of applesauce on the table and took her seat, she heard Corky muttering, "What's on the porch— what's on the porch . . ."

"Hurry, Corky!" she said.

"What'll I bring?" Corky called. "The washing machine? The egg crate? Or Aunt Willa's overshoes?"

"Silly!" she called back. "Look on the shelf. On the racks."

In a moment Corky entered the dining room carrying one cookie on the plate.

"Corky!" Monica scolded, wondering what joke he was playing now. "Bring enough for everybody. Bring lots of 'em. Leave just enough for supper."

"My dear young lady!" said Corky. "We'll have to get together on this. I've brought all there are."

"Oh, Corky!" she scoffed good-naturedly, and, snatching the plate from him, she hurried to the porch. In a moment she returned, her blue eyes smoldering.

"Who ate—Doak, did you and Benny eat those cookies?" she demanded.

With the lone cookie on the plate, she stood looking accusingly at Doak and Benny. Then, in spite of her efforts to control her feelings, tears welled in her eyes and splashed hotly down her cheeks.

"They were good, Corky!" she sobbed, and wiped her eyes on her arm.

"Doak!" Corky could make his voice sizzle when he wanted to, and it sizzled now. "Did you and Benny eat the cookies?"

"Yes, sir."

"All right," he said. "This afternoon you'll make it up to Monica. What'll be the punishment?"

An awkward silence followed.

"We'll help you wash the dishes, Monica," Doak volunteered meekly.

"We'll wash 'em by ourselves," Benny offered for good measure.

Monica sniffed back her tears and looked at the contrite faces.

"Is that satisfactory, Monica?" Corky asked.

"Sure. That'll be all right."

"See that you wash them properly, boys," Corky warned. "This was a dinner I'll never forget, Monica," he added, heartily. "It was flavored with do-or-die, and that's a flavor that's hard to beat." He took his straw hat from a hook on Bridget's Porch and started out the door. "Say!" he called back. "How about stirring up another batch of cookies some time? Some rainy day when I'm in the house to stand guard? The sample looks larrupin'."

Dutifully and contritely, Doak and Benny pushed back their chairs and set to work carrying dishes to the kitchen.

"I'll wash," chose Doak.

"I'll wipe," said Benny.

"Why don't you sit down and talk to us, Monica?" invited Doak.

"Here," offered Benny. "I'll put a chair by the door for you where it's cooler."

Monica sat by the door in the hot breeze, like an uneasy queen on a throne, and watched as Doak dripped soapy dish-water about on the floor, and Benny trailed the dish cloth from sink to cabinet.

"Get a smaller cloth out of the cabinet drawer, Benny," she suggested. "That one's Uncle Steve's size. And, Doak, leave the dishrag in the pan when you go for more dishes. Don't hang it on the side of the sink to drip. Then you won't have so much floor to mop."

They obeyed as if her word were pleasant law. And, as they worked, they talked, talked, talked, mainly about fan-tail pigeons.

"We're going to hatch lots of baby fantails," Doak said, dawdling with the silverware.

"You never did see a baby fantail, Monicky?" asked Benny.

"Never," said Monica.

"Shucks, man! They're the cutest things alive!" Doak told her.

"I expect we'll have as many baby fantails as Aunt Willa has baby chickens," prophesied Benny, quite overstepping the possible.

"When are you going to get your fantails?" asked Monica.

"When we get enough money," said Doak. "Twenty-five cents more apiece. Then we can get them. Say," he looked at Monica, "why don't we go to see them this afternoon? As soon as we take the lemonade to the field?"

"Sure!" agreed Benny. "Why don't we?"

"You go with us, Monica," invited Doak. "All three of us can ride Firefly."

"All three of us?"

"Sure. Seven could ride her if they wanted to," boasted Benny.

Monica leaned back in her chair and studied them. Their exaggeration was matched only by their youthful generosity. The afternoon was going to be long, and hot. It would be nice to jog down to Caseyville by the river, see the wondrous fantails, and jog back again.

She wondered what Aunt Willa would do with two boys who had disrupted a house for a whole morning, had failed to bring apples for the pie, and had eaten up the cookies.

"When you have enough money to buy the fantails, I'll go with you for them," she said. "But this afternoon we've got something else to do."

"What?" they asked suspiciously.

"As soon as you've taken the lemonade, you're to help me make another batch of cookies."

"Oh, Monicky!" they groaned. "You don't mean it!"

"Yes, I do," she said. "Or maybe we'll try cupcakes this time instead of cookies," she added in an effort to undergird their sagging spirits. "I'll let you make colored icing for them. I know where Aunt Willa keeps the coloring. And at suppertime you may serve them yourselves and surprise everybody. Right?"

There was silence while the boys weighed her proposition.

"Green icing," chose Doak, with only lukewarm enthusiasm.

"Pink," said Benny.

CHAPTER SIX

The Ghost of Dreams

On Wednesday morning, after the haying was finished, Monica, Nancy, and Corky walked together to the barn before breakfast to do their chores. The sun was up ahead of them, scorching and burning the already hard-baked earth. The coarse cottonwood leaves that flapped nervously in the slightest breeze hung motionless in the morning heat, and the screechings of the cicadas even at that early hour were like volleys of whining bullets fired at the dry, feverish hills.

Harlan and Coralie had dropped by the evening before. On the Kinfolks Porch, in the soft darkness, while lightning bugs had circled and sparkled like celestial pinwheels over the lawn, Harlan had laid his decisions before Uncle Steve. The cattle could take the drought no longer, he had said. The time had come to sell them.

Corky opened the barnyard gate, and Monica and Nancy passed through, carrying their milk buckets. Inside the barnyard, Monica paused a minute, listening to the cattle bawl.

91

"At least," she confided to Corky, "we'll get rid of this bawling when the cattle are sold."

"Monica," advised Corky, "think again. You might think of something besides the bawling the Fifers will be without when the cattle are sold."

"I don't deserve that!" Monica defended herself stoutly.

Corky was too busy with his own thoughts to answer her. He disappeared into the barn. This morning, Monica noted, he wasn't whistling.

Nancy, too, was quiet. Before milking, she fed T-Bone his special rations, and she stroked his neck and petted him as she did every morning. But she left off her usual flattering monologue in praise of his excellence.

As Monica milked, her mind was full of questions. But neither Corky nor Nancy, she sensed, welcomed questions. Corky was glum as he opened the corral gate a crack to let the young calves in for their breakfast. And any questions asked in Nancy's direction, Monica decided, would glance off her back and fall to the ground unheeded.

She was grateful when Uncle Steve, at breakfast, discussed the day's activities openly.

"You and Harlan got the corral fence mended, Corky?" he asked. "The cattle in the mood they're in will go right through a weak spot."

"We're going over it first thing after breakfast," replied Corky.

"Since Harlan's made a deal with Jarvis to use his truck," said Uncle Steve, "you ought to get the cattle to Evansville easily in two days by using three trucks."

"Ten head to a truck. Twelve truck loads," estimated Corky. "That is, if Harlan sells only the hundred and twenty he says he's going to sell."

"Looks like he ought to be able to weather the others over on green cornstalks till fall if he has to," said Uncle Steve. "By that time we should have had enough rain to get a good stand of Balbo rye. But it'll take a lot of cornstalks to tide over the forty cows and forty calves and those twenty young cattle he plans to keep."

"And a lot of water, too, Uncle Steve," Corky reminded him. "The ponds are drying up so fast that, if this drought keeps up much longer, there won't be any left. Even the big pond back of the barn is getting pretty low."

"Before all the ponds dry up, you'd better begin hauling water to the cattle from the pump in the barnyard," said Uncle Steve. "Luckily that well has never run dry."

As soon as Corky finished breakfast, he took Uncle Steve's handsaw, hammer, and nails from the tool shed, and set out for the corral on the west side of the barn. Harlan met him there, and for an hour they worked at mending the wooden fence that surrounded the corral. For the first time Monica realized that the real purpose of the corral was something other than penning up small calves at milking time. When she had finished her share of the morning chores, she walked out on the Kinfolks Porch to watch, and to listen to the final hammering that echoed against the hills.

"Where's Nancy, Aunt Willa?" she called back to the kitchen, remembering that she hadn't seen Nancy since breakfast.

"I believe she went up to her room," answered Aunt Willa. "I haven't seen her."

"You know what's different about this summer?" Monica asked a minute later as she stood in the kitchen doorway.

Aunt Willa was briskly shining her already immaculate

stove. At Monica's question she looked up quickly, as if she had been startled from some reverie.

"What's different?" Aunt Willa paused with her hand on the stove, and for a moment considered the question.

"In a way, everything's different, Monica. When you shut out all other summers and see only this one, and mark the ruin of the drought, everything's different. But, if you look at this summer as one in a long parade of summers, nothing much is different. Why did you ask me that? What makes this summer different for you?"

"All those beans, remember?" said Monica. "And blackberries. And tomatoes. And cabbages."

Aunt Willa smiled wanly at her.

"When we remember those summers," she said, "I feel as if I should like to begin bawling, like the cattle." And she went back to shining the stove as if her busyness helped her to forget.

If nobody was in a mood for conversation, Monica decided, she might as well write letters. She brought her stationery and sat in the swing on the Kinfolks Porch. But she never got so far as writing a letter. She never unscrewed her pen, in fact, but busied herself looking out over Nancy's burned garden.

In earlier summers, during the month of June, and well into July, she and Nancy and Aunt Willa had been as busy in the garden and the kitchen as ever the men were in the hayfield. It had been her job and Nancy's to pick the fresh vegetables and to help Aunt Willa in the kitchen as she canned, or preserved, or processed them for freezing for the winter's use. One day it was beans that Monica and Nancy picked by the baskets full and brought to Bridget's Porch— wax beans of pale green-gold, pencil-like green beans, and the gangly, tender pods of Kentucky Wonders, arching long and full-flavored from their tent poles. The next day it was sweet corn that they gathered in gunny sacks. The third day it was lima beans, and green beans again. The next day it was cabbage to be shredded and made into kraut. By the following day, the beans were ready for picking again. At odd times there were okra, carrots, and beets. And in the lower end of the garden, tomatoes were ripening, while along the fence rows on the hillside back of the house blackberries in luscious, jeweled clumps waited to be picked and made into tangy jams and rich, dark jellies.

This summer, however, the blades on Nancy's corn curled in the heat, and scarcely an ear formed on the tasseled stalks. The bean blossoms dried up, faded, and fell to the ground without forming pods; the green tomatoes dropped off the vines; and the beets and carrots were held by the hard-baked earth as in a vise. And though the blackberries on the hillsides had produced their clusters of pure white blossoms, such berries as formed dried up and shrank to wizened knots on the bushes.

Monica laid her stationery and pen in the swing. Jumping down from the porch, she walked across the yard to the garden fence to inspect her zinnias. Even though she had watered them diligently until they had taken root, they now seemed sick of the burning, unquenchable fever that afflicted all vegetation. Not one centerpiece had they produced. Instead, the few sickly blooms on the stalks were turning brown in spots and patches.

Monica felt herself recoiling from the shock of seeing dying zinnias preserved, upright and blooming. They were like a row of dry, brown ghosts, standing where white and gold flowers were to have bloomed for the Fifer table. So were the dreams in the Fifer house like dry, brown ghosts, she reflected—Nancy's dream of college and Harlan's dream of successful farming. The drought had burned the life out of the dreams, but their ghostly shapes were everywhere she looked, reminding her how fair their promise had been.

For a moment Monica's gaze strayed beyond her garden to Nancy's. For a moment, too, she tried hard to feel that the drought was a tragedy in her own life, as well as in Nancy's. But nothing really depended on her garden, she knew, and it had never actually claimed her as Aunt Willa had planned that it should. How, then, could she be expected to taste the full bitterness of the drought? How could anyone taste bitterness, she asked herself, who hadn't been forced to a bitter diet?

As she stood thinking, a movement to the west caught her eye. Cattle were coming along the high graveled road toward the Fifer corral, driven by Corky and Harlan, Cowboy Mullins and the other hired man, all on horseback.

The bawling of the cattle caught the attention of Uncle Steve, who was sitting in his chair under the maples. Without a word, he turned his chair and wheeled it to the fence beside Monica. Together they watched as the lean cattle moved slowly and clumsily along the road, kicking up a thick cloud of yellow dust that almost enveloped the horseback riders, and filling the countryside with their bawling. Now and then, the voice of one of the men rose higher than the continuous volume of bawling as commands were shouted, and threats were flung at would-be runaways from the herd.

On the cattle came, a dark-red herd with sober white faces, trampling in the dust all of Harlan's dreams, and laying on his young shoulders the heavy burden of debt in which he had involved the other Fifers as well.

"Do you know the hardest part of being a father, Monica?" asked Uncle Steve quietly. He seemed to be talking not so much to Monica as to himself. "It's having to stand by helpless, hands off, and watch your children carry their own loads. And being afraid the loads are too heavy for them."

In silence they watched Corky ride around the cattle and head them into the private lane leading to the barn and the corral. Aunt Willa left the kitchen, and came to stand on the Kinfolks Porch to watch. Doak and Benny came from the pond back of the barn and climbed on the fence to see the cattle being herded into the corral.

Most of the day Harlan, Corky, and the hired men worked with the cattle, herding all of them from the three pastures into the corral, and there separating those to be kept from those to be sold. By evening milking time the hundred to be kept were milling about in the pasture back of the barn. But having nothing to eat, they huddled near the corral fence, and together with the corraled cattle set up a raucous din with their bawling that caused Monica to milk furiously in order to finish quickly and put some distance between her and the frightful noise.

Aunt Willa came to the barn at milking time, looking for Harlan. When she found him, she had to shout into his ear to make herself heard.

"I want you to go home and get Coralie," she told him. "You're to have supper with us."

Monica watched Harlan get into his car and start for Coralie. He behaved numbly, as if he did without thinking whatever Aunt Willa told him to do.

At the supper table, Aunt Willa tried to keep a conversation going, but it was hard to hear, or even to think, above the bawling of the cattle. Only Uncle Steve came to her assistance, but his customary cheerfulness was not contagious. The young Fifers were in no mood for cheerfulness.

"Benny, you'd better eat your supper," Aunt Willa reminded him when, at a time everyone else's plate was almost empty, his food remained untouched.

At her warning, Benny broke into loud crying. "How'd you like to be that hungry?" he sobbed.

"Come here, Benny," said Uncle Steve.

Benny left his place and stumbled to the head of the table.

"You see, my boy," Uncle Steve explained, with his arm about Benny, "tomorrow the cattle are going to Evansville. And somebody there will buy them—some farmer from Indiana, or Illinois, or Ohio. And he'll take Harlan's cattle to his farm that hasn't been burned up in a drought. And he'll drive his truck right out into his pasture where the grass is green and thick, and a cool stream is flowing. Then he'll fasten a ramp to the truck. And he'll open up the back end of his truck and the cattle will walk down the ramp and out into the pasture, and they'll eat, and eat, and drink, and drink. And they'll never bawl again because they're hungry or thirsty. Now, you run gobble up Aunt Willa's good supper, because Harlan might need you and Doak to sit on the fence in the morning and help the men load. See?"

It was surprising, Monica noticed, how much better the food seemed to taste to everyone after that. It was surprising, too, how Aunt Willa and Coralie chatted away at dishwashing as if the operation scheduled for morning were nothing to worry about. Only Nancy had little to contribute to the conversation.

"Ready to go, Coralie?" Harlan asked as soon as the womenfolks joined the men in the living room.

"When are you going to start loading, Harlan?" Corky asked.

"As soon as we can see," said Harlan. "Figure we'll have to make four trips. If we get an early start in the morning, we might be able to make three trips tomorrow. Want to get the cattle on the market before the price drops any lower."

"We can't get in four round trips tomorrow?" asked Corky, looking out across the starlit darkness toward the corral.

The bawling of the hungry cattle was like a sea of raging sound, rising now here, now there, in frenzied waves that spent themselves in ceaseless roar and rumble.

"I'd like to," said Harlan. "The wheat's waiting for us. But I think we'll need two days. Or one and a half."

"We'd better turn in early tonight," said Uncle Steve.

Reaching for the Bible, he quietly thumbed the leaves in search of the passage he wished to read.

Lord,
Thou hast been our dwelling place in all generations.
Before the mountains were brought forth,
or ever Thou hadst formed the earth and the world,
even from everlasting to everlasting,
Thou art God.

In the corral the hungry cattle bawled their misery to the starry skies, and in the treetops the cicadas dinned their screeching chorus. But against the raucous noise, Uncle Steve's voice was steady and deep-toned and sure, making safe the little island where the Fifers dwelt in the midst of ruin.

Let the beauty of the Lord our God be upon us;
and establish Thou the work of our hands upon us;
yea, the work of our hands establish Thou it.

Quietly Uncle Steve laid aside the book. When Harlan
and Coralie rose to go, he got to his feet. With a crutch under
one arm, he placed a hand on Harlan's shoulder and walked
out on the Kinfolks Porch with them and to the steps.

"Good night, children. Sleep well tonight."

It was a gentle benediction that all the Fifers took to bed
with them, but Monica, lying awake in the hot bedroom
beside Nancy and hearing the cattle bawling, felt the effects
of it wearing off. She wanted to talk to Nancy. Nancy was
awake, she knew. No one could possibly be asleep who was
lying as still as Nancy, as defiantly, stiffly still—so still that
Monica didn't dare speak to her. Maybe, Monica thought,
cotton in her ears would deaden the sound of the bawling.

She was about to bestir herself to slip out of bed and go
to the bathroom in search of cotton when she thought of
Uncle Steve. He didn't have cotton in his ears, she wagered.
Neither did Aunt Willa. They had no need of cotton in their
ears. Nor of aspirin tablets. Why, she thought, not even
Nancy had cotton in her ears. She was lying there being tor-
tured by the thought of having to give up college. But she
was taking her torture straight.

Suddenly Monica realized a new respect for Nancy—a
respect that grew, and deepened like a sunset afterglow.

Monica sensed as soon as she opened her eyes the next
morning that she had awaked no later than usual. Yet Nancy
was up and gone.

Bounding out of bed, Monica hustled into her clothes, ran
downstairs, snatched up a milk bucket from the shelf on

Bridget's Porch, and hurried to the barn. She discovered Nancy there ahead of her, her head pressed close against the flank of the cow she was milking.

Monica studied her a second. Her posture, she decided, didn't invite conversation.

She went for a milking stool and stopped for a moment to look at the cattle in the corral. She had expected to see the men there loading them for market, but no one seemed to be around except Nancy.

Seating herself on her stool, she began milking.

"Have they gone, Nancy?" she asked after a moment.

"Half an hour ago," Nancy muttered.

Monica bent to her milking, keeping in mind the happy lot of the cattle now on their way to market as Uncle Steve had pictured it to Benny the evening before. In spite of the bawling of the cattle yet to go to Evansville, she felt unusually cheerful.

"Even if selling the cattle does mean losing money, everything's going to be all right in the end, isn't it, Nancy?" she asked.

Nancy did not reply.

Monica rose quietly from her stool and peered over the back of the cow she was milking. There was something mysterious about Nancy's silence, she thought as she watched her cousin, something defiant about the furious way she was milking.

She glanced at T-Bone's pen in a corner of the barnyard. The pen was empty.

Once again, she settled herself on her stool and began milking. But her cheerfulness was now clouded with a strange uneasiness. Where was T-Bone, she wondered.

Plagued by the question, she got to her feet once more,

and on a pretense left her milking and went into the barn. Sometimes, she remembered, Nancy shut T-Bone in a stall.

In a dim stall, smelling strongly of antiseptic, Monica found the prized calf. She glanced at him, and gasped. He was standing on three legs on the earthen floor of the stall. The knee of his right front leg was swollen almost twice its normal size. His once sleek hair was matted where blood had flowed from a long gash on his shoulder. His face was battered, and disfigured with clotted blood. He looked piteously at Monica out of pain-clouded eyes.

"Nancy!" cried Monica, running outside. "What happened to T-Bone?"

Nancy didn't look up from her milking. "He got out of his pen in the night," she said, her voice lifeless. "The mules bit him and kicked him."

Monica stood staring at her. Why was she being so calm, she wondered. Why wasn't she doing something?

"Why don't you call the vet?" she asked.

"The vet's been here already," Nancy told her.

"What did he say?" asked Monica.

Without answering, Nancy stripped the cow she was milking, and moved to another, carrying her stool with her. Her eyes, too, were full of pain, like T-Bone's, Monica noticed.

"Can he—T-Bone'll be all right, won't he?" Monica asked, apprehensively.

"It's no use trying to save him," Nancy told her, the lifelessness of her voice betraying the great effort she was making to control it. "Harlan's taking T-Bone to Evansville on the next load."

"Oh, Nancy!" Monica felt weak and sick as she reflected on this newest tragedy heaped on top of other tragedies. "I'm sorry, Nancy," she said, her voice close to tears.

Nancy did not answer. Steadily she milked away, keeping her head buried against the flank of the cow. The sound of the milk in the foam reminded Monica that she, too, had milking to do.

As soon as Nancy had finished milking, she poured milk into the kittens' pan, and, without a word, went to the house alone, leaving Monica behind.

When Monica arrived at the house, she found Aunt Willa putting breakfast on the table.

"Do you know about T-Bone, Aunt Willa?" she asked.

"Yes, my dear," answered Aunt Willa.

"Can't the vet do something for him?"

"He's done all he can," explained Aunt Willa. "He came to the house and talked to your Uncle Steve and me. T-Bone's been so badly crippled that he stands no chance at all in a show ring, and the vet advises selling him now along with the other cattle."

"Then Nancy will get some money from him?" asked Monica.

"Some. The regular market price."

Monica strained the milk from her bucket into the separator.

"I'm awfully sorry, Aunt Willa," she said.

"We're all sorry, Monica," Aunt Willa told her. "It isn't easy for a girl to watch one prop after another pulled out from under her plans. Are you ready for breakfast?"

"In a minute."

Taking the stairs two at a time, Monica dashed upstairs to brush her hair. Inside the doorway of the room she stopped short. Across the unmade bed lay Nancy, face down. Her body was jerking with big, uncontrollable sobs.

"Nancy!" cried Monica.

The sobbing continued.

Softly Monica walked to the foot of the bed and stood looking down at her cousin.

"I'm awfully sorry, Nancy," she said.

"Oh, shut up! And go away!" stormed Nancy. "You don't know what it's like. You never had to give up anything in your whole life!"

Monica turned. Quietly she crossed the room, shut the door behind her, and went soberly downstairs. Later, when she carried upstairs the tray on which Aunt Willa had placed Nancy's breakfast, she found Nancy still lying on the bed, but her crying, like a storm, had spent itself.

Monica made room for the tray on the bedside table.

"Here's your breakfast, Nancy," she said, invitingly.

When Nancy made no move, Monica started toward the door.

"I'm sorry for what I said, Monica," mumbled Nancy, with the sound of tears still in her voice.

"Forget it," advised Monica. "I have."

Back in the kitchen she washed and dried the breakfast dishes.

"Does losing T-Bone mean that Nancy can't go to college at all, Aunt Willa?" she asked, thoughtfully.

"Not necessarily," said Aunt Willa.

"But the fact that Uncle Steve has lost his money on the cattle, and Nancy's garden's burned up, too, is going to make it pretty hard for her, isn't it?"

"Hard, yes," agreed Aunt Willa. "Getting through college won't be easy. But when all of us put our heads together, we'll surely find a way."

"She's taking this awfully hard about T-Bone," said Monica.

"She hates to part with T-Bone, especially this way," Aunt Willa told her. "Poor child! She'd taken such good care of him!"

"Remember the day we went to town for the zinnias, and you said Nancy didn't know everything about the Fifer way of life? We were talking about poetry in farming, remember?"

"Yes, I remember," said Aunt Willa. "To know some things you have to taste them. Like an apple. You can't really know what an apple's like until you taste it. And you can't know what missing out on college might be like until you can't see any way to get there."

As Monica put away the dishes she had dried, she was thinking busily not only of Nancy, but of Harlan and Coralie, and of Uncle Steve, and of the destruction the drought was working on the Fifer farm.

"This is a dark day for everybody, isn't it, Aunt Willa?" she asked.

"Yes," said Aunt Willa, "it is. But it's only one day. It isn't all our lives—not all of Harlan's nor all of Nancy's. It isn't even the most important day of our lives. It's just a day that like all the others will have to be woven in as smoothly as we can weave it."

"Why don't you tell Nancy that?" asked Monica.

"Nancy is too stunned to hear it now," said Aunt Willa. "But sometime she'll listen. How would you and Doak and Benny like to stir up another batch of cupcakes this morning? Your others were very good."

"Sure," agreed Monica. "They love to make the frosting. They go in for bright colors."

"Bright colors will be fine," declared Aunt Willa. "They'll fit right in with an idea I've just had."

"What is it?" asked Monica.

"Harlan ought to be through hauling the cattle by to-morrow noon," said Aunt Willa. "Then he'll want the after-noon to get the combine in shape for wheat harvest. What would you think of our going to the river for a picnic sup-per? Harlan and Coralie, your Uncle Steve, Nancy, every-body. We could fix lots of fried chicken and potato salad. You could drive me into town this afternoon for lettuce and tomatoes and olives."

"May we have a watermelon, too?" asked Monica.

"Sure!" agreed Aunt Willa. "We can make a freezer of ice cream in the morning, too."

Footsteps sounded on the Kinfolks Porch.

"Doak!" called Monica. "Benny! That you?"

"Yep," called Doak.

"How would you boys like to help me make some more cupcakes this morning?" asked Monica as they entered the kitchen.

"Green icing," chose Doak.

"Know what, Monicky?" said Benny. "I'm going to take every color Aunt Willa has and mix them up together."

"Fine, Benny!" said Monica. "Let's give those cupcakes the works!"

CHAPTER SEVEN

One Way to Miss a Circus

The selling of the cattle brought a change to the Fifer household. The days and, more especially, the nights were no longer filled with frenzied bawling since now Corky daily spread on the hillsides a truck load of earless green cornstalks for the cattle that remained.

Another change could be neither seen nor heard, but every Fifer sensed it. The drought had demanded a costly sacrifice of them, but, in making the sacrifice, they had also made their peace with the weather. It had done its worst to them, and they were no longer afraid of it. They could wait out the drought now until fall, until the time for sowing Balbo rye for fall pasturage. It was a long time to wait, but no one doubted that by that time the drought would be broken.

"If I can find some snow fence any place," Harlan said as he lay on the river bank resting after the picnic, "we can build a temporary silo and put the cornstalks in it before they dry up completely. That way we can save something from the crop. Feed it to the cattle this winter."

"A snow-fence silo?" questioned Corky.

"Snow fence and tar paper," said Harlan. "Sure, we can keep ensilage that way. We'll get at it as soon as the wheat's combined." He rolled on his back and looked up at the clear sky. "Thanks, Mom, for this new lease on life before we start on the wheat."

"How long will the wheat harvest take, do you think?" asked Uncle Steve.

"Through next week, probably," said Harlan.

"It ought to be a fairly good harvest," predicted Uncle Steve. "The wheat was pretty well along before the drought hit it."

"We can stay with it every night," said Harlan, in the manner of one who is planning aloud. "No dew to hinder."

Harlan and Corky were already in the first of the wheat fields the next morning when Monica and Nancy went to milk. Corky must have been up before day, they decided, for the cattle were eating ravenously of the green cornstalks he had already cut that morning and spread out for them on the hillside pasture back of the barn.

In mid-morning, Monica, riding Firefly, took a jug of lemonade to the harvesters. The wheat chosen to be harvested first grew in a broad hollow at the far edge of the farm. On top of the ridge overlooking the field, Monica stopped Firefly and looked down on the busy scene—on Harlan and Corky working tensely, on the burnished wheat, and on the wind. She fancied she could see the form of the hot wind as it lashed against the wheat and sent great, broad golden wave after wave down the hollow.

"Hey, Monica!" Corky's voice rose above the clatter of

the machinery and was carried to her on a wave of wind.
"Get down here with that lemonade!"

Monica clucked to Firefly and dug her heels into the
mare's ribs. As she rode down the slope and across the
stretch of stubble, she watched Harlan and Corky at work—
Harlan, eyes straightforward, in too much of a hurry, as Aunt
Willa said, riding the tractor down the field, never wasting
a minute; and Corky, shirtless and wearing a broad-brimmed
straw hat on his head, standing on the combine platform and
sewing the coarse sacks as fast as the cataract of golden
kernels filled them.

As she approached, Harlan raised his eyes from the sea of
gold and stopped the tractor. Monica, sitting on Firefly,
poured the lemonade into the plastic glasses she had
brought, and handed them to Harlan and Corky. Twice she
filled the glasses, three times, and four times.

"Thanks, Monica," Harlan said as he drained the fourth
glass. "Ready, Corky?"

"You bet!" replied Corky, handing his glass to Monica.
"And you, you gallop straight home and bring us more lemonade. We're so parched that this evaporates before it hits
bottom."

And away went the combine, hungrily gathering in on one
side the burnished heads of wheat, and from the other side
spilling forth the husked grains in a golden cataract.

Day after day, with only Sunday for a rest day, the gruelling wheat harvest went on. Because of the absence of dew,
the men were in the fields soon after daybreak, and, with
only brief pauses for meals, they worked until ten o'clock
in the evening, harvesting in the glare of spotlights.

At mealtime Corky was so tired that he ate glumly, and,
when finally he came home in the evening, he slumped on

the floor with his back against the doorframe and dozed as Uncle Steve read from the Bible. When the reading was finished, he pulled himself up, splashed hastily through a warm bath, and fell into bed "more dead than alive," Aunt Willa said, shaking her head over him. It was as if, out of deference to his weariness, no one else talked much at the table, either—deference to him, and to Nancy who seemed to have little life or ambition left in her.

Except for the milking morning and evening, and the daily chores about the house, Nancy had found little to fill her time. Her calf and garden gone, she had nothing to claim her, nothing to work for, nothing to chart. Each day she disappeared into her room for hours at a time, and offered no explanations. And each day, more and more, she clammed up and kept her thoughts to herself.

On the next to the last day of the wheat harvest, after Doak and Benny had brought the mail from the box at the end of the lane, Monica sat in the swing on the Kinfolks Porch and read the newspaper.

"Hey, Nancy!' she called. "There's going to be a circus in Evansville tomorrow. Let's go."

"What for?" asked Nancy.

"Why, to see it, of course."

"I don't feel like circuses," said Nancy, after a pause.

"Seeing it might make you feel better," suggested Monica.

"Besides, what do we use for money?" asked Nancy.

"Listen," said Monica. "Remember my weekly letter that came from Dad yesterday had my monthly allowance in it. I've got enough to pay our bus fare up there, buy our circus tickets, and everything. I've got enough even for side shows."

"Better keep it," advised Nancy. "A drought might hit

you. But, of course," she added pointedly, "you don't have to depend on zinnias to get you to college."

Monica glanced through the wire fence at her garden.

Her zinnias were still standing tall and straight, each with a flower on the top of the stalk, but dead from petal tip to root. They checked her impulse to retort to Nancy that her temper needed improving. She went back to reading about the circus, silently.

Before long, Doak and Benny came sauntering around the corner of the porch.

"Hey, kids," called Monica, "how'd you like to go to a circus?"

"A circus?" asked Doak. "Where?"

"When?" asked Benny.

"Tomorrow at Evansville," Monica told them.

"Gee!" sighed Doak.

"Gee whiz!" sighed Benny.

"If Aunt Willa will let us go, I'll pay all our expenses," offered Monica. "I've got enough money from my allowance."

"Let's ask her," suggested Benny.

Together they went in search of Aunt Willa. They found her at the sewing machine, mending sheets. The sight of her employment gave Monica a start. Maybe, she reflected, the Fifers would get well acquainted with patches and mends before they recovered fully from the effects of the drought. Monica outlined their plans to Aunt Willa.

"And we'll get back home safe and sound, won't we, Monicky?" Benny added as Monica finished.

His words started a train of memory in Monica's mind. Aunt Willa hadn't trusted her to get across Evansville alone when she first came. Would she now trust her not only to take care of herself in Evansville, but to look after Doak and Benny as well?

"I really can find my way around all right, Aunt Willa," she argued persuasively. "At home Daddy lets me go downtown alone. And I promise I'll let nothing happen to Doak and Benny."

Aunt Willa fitted edges of the sheet together as she studied Monica's request.

"When you meet the seven o'clock bus in Colgate, you'll see us stepping off just the way we stepped on in the morning," persuaded Monica.

"Only, of course, we will have seen the circus," amended Doak.

"Of course," added Benny.

"I don't like you to spend so much of your money, Monica," Aunt Willa objected, thoughtfully.

"But I have all of ten dollars," said Monica. "And there doesn't seem to be any other way to spend it."

Aunt Willa looked at her affectionately. "My dear," she said, "we've been so engrossed in all our troubles that we haven't seen to it at all that a girl has a little fun, have we?"

"Oh, no, Aunt Willa, it isn't that," Monica hastened to assure her. "It just seemed like—well, here's a circus, and who wants to miss a circus?"

"I don't," said Doak.

"I know I don't," said Benny.

"Maybe Doak and Benny would be willing to use part of their pigeon money for their tickets," suggested Aunt Willa.

"No siree," Doak and Benny remonstrated.

"I don't want them to," said Monica. "I want to pay their way myself."

"If your Uncle Steve thinks it's all right," said Aunt Willa, "why you may go."

Uncle Steve listened with a twinkle in his eyes as they outlined their plans to him.

"If I were a doctor, Willa," he declared, "a circus is just what I'd order for these three." And he told Doak and Benny stories of clowns, of gymnasts and bareback riders, of trained elephants and seals and pythons—stories that sent them rolling on the brown grass with laughter or left them speechless with wonder.

The next morning, the circus goers were driven into Colgate by Aunt Willa and Uncle Steve to catch the early morning bus to Evansville. They crowded into the vacant front seat of the bus, and waved an excited farewell through the window.

"Be home at seven," Monica framed with her lips. When Aunt Willa's puzzled expression indicated she didn't understand, Doak shouted through the air slots, "Be home at seven!"

As the big bus bore them swiftly along the hot highway toward Evansville, Monica felt as excited as her two young cousins. She leaned back in the seat and listened to their incessant chatter. The importance to them of everything they saw seemed blown up to monstrous size—the people who boarded the bus at way stations, the dazzling announcements of the circus posted on the walls of a roadside tobacco barn, the big Ohio River bridge and the massive girders past which they zing-zing-zing-zinged. It was only as the bus was pulling into the Evansville station and passengers were dragging their bags from overhead that Monica realized her own excitement must be tempered with responsibility.

"I think we'll take a city bus and go straight to the circus grounds," she explained to the boys. "The circus doesn't really start till after lunch, but the elephants will be there. Oh, we can see lots of things outside the big tent," she said, feeding their mounting excitement.

They took their stand on the hot street corner where the policeman in the bus station had told them to catch a city bus for the circus, and in ten minutes they were on their way. In another half hour they alighted from the bus at the edge of the city. There they found themselves part of a crowd of excited people, all circus-bent, even at that hour of the morning, and as part of the crowd they hurried across vacant lots and along a dusty roadway to the circus lot. Everywhere, in every direction, were sounds of hammering and shouting as men and women prepared for the big show.

"Where're the clowns?" asked Benny in an awed voice.

"They're working, like everybody else," explained Monica. "You can't tell the clowns from anybody else now."

"Let's go see the elephants," urged Doak.

On the far side of the lot they found the elephants, and for almost an hour, with Doak holding one hand and Benny the other, Monica led them in front of the elephants, and watched with them as the elephants tossed straw with their trunks and scooped up peanuts thrown to them.

"It's eleven o'clock, boys," Monica said finally, consulting her watch. "Why don't we go back across the grounds where the hot dog stands are and eat our lunch now? Then we'll be ready to buy our tickets as soon as they go on sale, and go inside the tent and get good seats."

Back through the growing crowd, in heat and dust they made their way, around the mammoth tent that had mushroomed since they arrived, to the other side of the circus grounds. Monica spotted a hot dog stand built sketchily of old lumber and covered with oilcloth, and led Doak and Benny toward it.

"Right this way to get your foot-long hot dogs!" a fat man with a chef's cap made of newspaper on his head and a dirty bib apron around his middle was shouting from the stand.

"Right here," said Monica to Doak and Benny.

She took her place at the foot of the line, still shepherding the boys by the hand, and moved up slowly to the make-shift counter. They watched fascinated as the fat man, like a clever magician, slit buns, plastered them with mustard, slapped hot dogs inside, wrapped paper napkins around them, and sent them spinning along the counter, one at a time, toward the customers.

"Hey, folks! Step right up this way to get your big foot-long hot dogs!" the fat man barked as sweat rolled down his face.

"Three hot dogs," ordered Monica when finally she reached the head of the line.

In record time the three hot dogs went spinning in their napkins along the counter toward Monica.

"Sixty cents," said the man. "Hey, folks!" he let his voice out. "Step this way to get your foot-long hot dogs! Sixty cents, lady. Move on."

While the boys stood enraptured with the antics of the fat man, and the noise and excitement of the crowd, Monica looked for her money to pay for the hot dogs. She remembered having put it carefully in her wallet, and having pushed the wallet deep into a pocket of the skirt she wore.

She felt in her right pocket. The wallet wasn't there. She felt in her left pocket. The wallet wasn't there.

She pulled her right pocket open as far as she could, and peered in. The wallet wasn't there.

"Hey, lady!" scolded the foot-long hot dog man. "Sixty cents. Get a move on."

"Just a minute," muttered Monica as she searched one pocket, then the other.

"What's the matter?" growled the man. "Got no money? Here," he addressed the next in line, "here're your hot dogs. Step out of line there, lady, till you find your money."

Dazedly Monica pulled Doak and Benny out of the line, and off at one side she went through a search of her pockets again. The wallet was nowhere to be found.

"Stay here a minute, boys," she told them, swallowing hard. She went back to the line, and walked slowly to the end of it, looking on the ground and about people's feet to see if she had dropped the wallet in line. But she couldn't find it.

"Doak," she said, as she rejoined the boys, her voice tight with fright, "have you seen my wallet, you or Benny?"

"When you bought our tickets in Colgate," said Doak.

"What did I do with it after I bought the tickets?" she asked.

"I don't know," said Doak.

"I don't know, either," said Benny. "Look in your pocket."

"I have looked, Benny," said Monica as she frantically looked again. "It's gone."

"Maybe somebody stole it," suggested Doak.

"Maybe a robber stole it," suggested Benny.

"I could have—have put it down some place, maybe," said Monica. She felt terror-stricken with the idea, and with the situation which she was beginning to realize had to be faced.

"Doak, I didn't give it to you, did I?" No sooner had the suggestion occurred to her than she dropped to her knees and began searching Doak's pockets. "Or you, Benny?" she asked, nervously searching Benny.

Taking the boys by the hand, Monica hurried them away from the crowd.

"Boys," she began, as she stopped and faced them. But realizing the consequences of her loss, she could not go on. She only stared at them dumbly.

"Can't we buy our hot dogs?" asked Doak.

She bit her lip and shook her head.

"Can't we buy our tickets to see the circus, either?" asked Benny.

She shook her head again.

"And that isn't the worst," she told them, after a moment, trying to steady her voice. "The worst is that—that we can't get home. Our return tickets are in the wallet, too."

"But we can telephone Corky," said Benny after a second's thought. "He'll come and get us."

"Sure!" Doak consoled her. "Corky'll come and get us, Monica. I bet you he'd like to come."

The thought of Corky coming to their rescue sent shivers of dread down Monica's spine. Still, she reminded herself, Corky had been pretty decent about the dinner she cooked. But that didn't mean he had any real confidence in her, she knew. He didn't think she knew how to do anything useful, or right. And maybe he wasn't far wrong. Else, why had she lost her money like a careless child?

"Why don't we telephone Corky, Monicky?" Benny urged her.

"Hush, Benny!" she said sharply.

The crowd was increasing now. Each time a city bus

arrived at the end of the line, it unloaded dozens of men and women and children, and boys the age of Doak and Benny who went hurrying excitedly across the field to see the elephants, and to watch the goings-on around the big tent.

"Can't we telephone Corky, Monica?" asked Doak.

"No," said Monica.

"What'll we do then?" asked Doak, his voice quivering with fright. He began to cry. Benny joined him.

"Boys," scolded Monica, "will you stop crying? I've got to think, and I can't think with you crying."

They wiped their eyes on their arms and looked at her wonderingly.

"Come with me," she said after another moment of thought, and started toward the hot dog stand. "Stay behind me. Try not to be seen."

She went around to the side of the hot dog stand, as far away from the line of customers as possible.

"Mister?" she called.

The foot-long hot dog man paid no attention.

"Mister!" she called louder.

He turned.

"Line's on this side," he gestured with his head and a hot dog. "Step right this away, folks, for your great big foot-long hot dogs."

"Mister, you could serve more if I came in there and helped you," called Monica.

"Come on in, then. What you waitin' for?" asked the man. "Just climb over the side. Step right up, folks!"

"What'll you pay me?" asked Monica.

"A hot dog," said the man.

"I have to be paid in money," said Monica.

"Business is bad, lady," the man told her, as he slashed buns and flung mustard on them. "It's a hot dog or nothin'. Take it or leave it. Thisaway, folks!"

"Will you make it three hot dogs?" bargained Monica.

"For an hour's work, yes," said the man. "That's whoppin' good pay. Sixty cents an hour."

"Stay right here," Monica whispered to Doak and Benny. "I'll get you a hot dog for your lunch." She stepped over the planks that formed the side of the booth.

"Can I have two hot dogs in advance?" she asked.

"One when you earn it," said the man. "Every twenty minutes. Here," he thrust a great butcher knife at her. "You cut buns and spread mustard. I'll lay on the dogs and collect the dough. Right thisaway, folks! Line's a movin' faster now."

With a quick look at her watch, Monica went to work, cutting buns open and plastering them with mustard, and glancing now and then at Doak and Benny who stood outside the booth looking as woebegone, she thought, as little lost orphans. When twenty minutes were up, she dabbed a bun with mustard and held it out to the man. "This one's for me," she told him.

"You can't eat on the job," he warned.

"I don't intend to," she answered. "It's for my two friends out there."

When he had laid a hot dog inside the bun, she broke bun and dog in the middle and handed them over the side of the booth to Doak and Benny. At the end of another twenty minutes, she repeated the performance. At the end of the hour, when she had collected another hot dog from the man, she said, "This one's for me. I'll be leaving now. And thanks a million."

"You can't leave now," stormed the man. "Look at all them customers waitin'."

"I'll work for money," Monica told him.

"I told you once, business is bad," he said.

"Sorry," said Monica. "I'll have to find another job." And taking the hot dog, she climbed over the side of the booth.

With Doak and Benny following her, Monica walked away from the crowd, back to the end of the bus line.

"Let's sit down here on the ground," she said, "while I eat my hot dog."

"What'll we do then?" asked Doak.

"Aren't we going to see the circus, Monicky?" begged Benny with boyish supplication in his voice. "That's what we came for."

"I'll try to think of some way," promised Monica. "Don't talk to me while I eat, but let me think. You think, too."

They sat quietly on stray pieces of newspaper Monica picked up from the ground, and as Monica ate, they thought. Monica thought about the kind old lady Aunt Willa had sent to help her transfer from train to bus. She could go down the street to somebody's house and telephone the woman, and the woman would come to their rescue. But then—what was the woman's name? Smith. That was it, Smith. But what Smith? If she hadn't been in such a surly mood that day Mrs. Smith met her, she might have learned which Mrs. Smith the woman was. A needle couldn't be harder to find in a haystack than Mrs. Smith in Evansville. And anyway, Mrs. Smith was probably at the circus.

"I can't see why we don't phone Corky," complained Doak.

"Sh-h!" said Monica. "I'm trying to think."

There was a long silence among the forlorn little group at the edge of the hurrying, excited crowd.

"Have you thought yet?" asked Benny finally.

"Yes, I have, Benny," said Monica, her voice small with the big fright that was inside her. "I'll have to find a job that'll pay us enough money to get us home."

"You mean we won't see the circus? The clowns and the acrobats?"

Monica couldn't face them. "I'm just as sorry as I know how to be, boys," she said. "But I'll do my best to get you home."

Her downcast eyes fell on the newspaper on which Benny was sitting. "Help Wanted—Women," ran the caption on the classified ad page.

She bent over and read, tracing the jobs down the column with her finger, through stenographers, bookkeepers, ladies to sell hats, ladies to sell hosiery, ladies to sell real estate, ladies to sell insurance, ladies to do domestic jobs. "Wanted: Woman to do ironing," she read. "3642 Belmont Street."

"Let me have this paper, Benny," she demanded, with excitement in her voice.

"Can you tell me where Belmont Street is?" she called to a man hurrying circusward with a small boy riding piggyback.

"That direction," he said, pointing north. "About six blocks. What number you want?"

"Thirty-six, forty-two," she told him.

"Two blocks this way," he pointed east.

"We going there?" asked Doak.

"Instead of to the circus?" asked Benny.

"I'll tell you what we'll do, boys," she said. "Let's go back close to the tent and see if I can find any sort of job that will pay me money. If I can't—well, let's try, shall we, and see what happens."

They tried. At a pop stand, at a cotton-candy stand, at a whirligig stand, at a pink lemonade stand, Monica asked for a job. But nobody had a job for her.

With the final no, she took the boys by the hand again and led them away from the big tent, away from the wonderful noise inside of drums beating and trumpets blaring and people shouting and laughing and clapping. Across the circus grounds they went, then six blocks north and two blocks east to 3642 Belmont Street.

In answer to her ring, an elderly woman came to the door —a woman with frowsy gray hair, a dour face that poorly concealed a lemon disposition, and a right arm in a sling.

"Yes?" she said, scowling.

"Did you advertise for somebody to iron for you?" asked Monica.

"Yes." The scowl deepened.

"How much do you pay for ironing?" Monica asked, shrinking before the woman.

"I pay in old clothes," said the woman.

"Oh!" said Monica, feeling her knees buckle under her weight. "Don't you ever pay money?"

"How much money do you want? You don't look like you've had much experience ironing. And who," she stared crossly down at Doak and Benny, "are these? I couldn't have them around every week."

"Oh, I don't want the job every week," explained Monica hastily. "I can only iron for you this afternoon. You see, we have to catch the five-thirty bus for home. We live at Colgate."

"And what in the world are you doing here?"

Monica told the old woman briefly the story of their plight.

"I may look inexperienced," she hastened to add, "but I'm a very good ironer. My Aunt Willa taught me how. And she's as particular as they come. To be a Fifer you have to be a good ironer. It's a family tradition."

The old woman's face looked just as sour as it had in the beginning. But her voice mellowed a little when she asked, "How much do you ask for ironing? I really need it done. It's all piled up since I broke my arm, and nobody seems to want to work nowadays."

Monica had already calculated her price—the cost of three city bus rides to the bus station and one whole ticket and two half tickets to Colgate.

"All right," said the woman, opening the door wide enough for them to enter. "Go to the kitchen. And see that these young uns keep quiet. I can't abide a lot of noise, my nerves are so shot."

Monica's heart sank when she saw the ironing piled high in a chair in the kitchen.

"Do you—did you want all that ironed?" she asked.

"Of course," said the woman. "What do you think I'm paying such a high price for? Plug your iron in here." She pointed to an outlet over the kitchen sink. "Here's your ironing board. And here's your sprinkling bottle."

When the old woman had left the kitchen, Monica drew a couple of chairs from under the kitchen table and placed them on the other side of the ironing board and facing her.

"Sit here, boys," she whispered, pointing to the chairs. "And don't move any more muscles than you have to."

Pushing back her hair from her hot, damp forehead, she pitched into the ironing. For an hour things went very well.

Monica was grateful to find most of the pieces flat—pillow cases and towels that must have been accumulating for a month. Even the old lady's dresses she was glad to see were on the plain side, with no frills and fancy pockets to iron.

Then the boys began to grow restless. They wanted to know the time of day. They asked how much more she had to iron, and when she would be through. They wanted to know if they couldn't go out and play. Benny thought he heard the band playing at the circus. What was wrong, he asked, with going back to the grounds and listening? They'd wait for her there.

"You can't go back, boys," she said. "You might get lost. You'll have to stay right here. And don't make noise, else we won't get home."

They endured for another half hour. Then Benny shoved Doak.

"Ow!" yelled Doak.

Monica set her iron down and glowered at them.

"You look just like her," tittered Benny, jerking his head in the direction of the front of the house.

It was then that Monica burst into tears.

"Aw, Monicky, I didn't mean it!" begged Benny.

Monica wiped her eyes. In that moment of relaxation, she realized that the kitchen with the sun beating on it from the west was unbearably hot, and that she was weary in every muscle. On top of that, she was frightened. And on top of the fright she was disgusted with herself, through and through, for getting them all into such a muddle.

"Monicky," Benny whispered, "you iron better even than Aunt Willa."

Monica felt like crying in earnest after this childish ministration of comfort. It was only by battling doggedly that she held back her tears and forced herself to think.

"I've got an idea," she whispered in a moment. "Would you boys like to earn enough this afternoon to buy your pigeons?"

They were alert at once, sitting questioningly on the edges of their chairs.

"How?" they asked.

"Wait a minute," she told them, and she disappeared in the direction the old lady had taken. In three minutes she was back.

"That old lemon face in there has a heart of gold," she whispered to them excitedly. "She says if you'll go outside and pick up every piece of paper and rubbish that's blown over the yard and into her shrubbery since she broke her arm, and put it in the garbage can in the back, she'll give each one of you a quarter."

"Is that enough to buy the fantails?" asked Doak.

"Exactly enough. That's all you lack."

"Can we go and get them tomorrow?"

"I suspect so."

"Will you go with us?" asked Benny.

"Do you want me to go?"

"Of course," said the boys together.

"All right," she promised. "Pick up every single smidgen of paper you can find in the yard. Show the old lady what Fifer boys are made of. You take one side of the yard, Doak, and you the other, Benny. Right?"

"Right," they agreed, and out the back door they tiptoed.

"We can hear the band out here, too," Benny put his head through the doorway to whisper.

"Fine!" said Monica.

It was easier to iron when the boys didn't have to be kept motionless in their chairs, and, as the kitchen clock over the sink flicked the quarter hours away, the stack of ironed clothes grew, and grew. By ten minutes of five the ironing was finished. The old woman counted out both Monica's and the boys' money in dimes and nickels from a little crystallized ginger box she took from a drawer. Monica hastily looked over the yard, pronounced the boys' work excellent, caught each of them by a hand, and raced for the city bus that would take them to the bus terminal.

When they were finally on the big bus and starting toward Colgate, the three of them crowded into a double seat as before, Monica glanced at Doak and Benny. They were very dirty. They were hungry, too. But they didn't seem unhappy.

"I'll bet Aunt Willa has a great big supper waiting for us," she said. "You know, boys, you did a swell job of that yard. And you—you—well, you're pretty swell, too."

They smiled wearily. But they didn't reply. Soon both heads began to droop.

"Stretch out and put your head against me," she said to Benny. "And, Doak, put your head against Benny."

Wearily they obeyed. Before they were across the river, both of them were sound asleep. And before they had gone a mile farther, Monica had joined them. It was not until the bus was nearing Colgate that they waked up.

"Shall we have a secret?" Monica asked as they stretched themselves and prepared to get off the bus. "Let's not tell the family we didn't see the circus. Let's let them find out."

Corky met them at the bus. Being Corky, he began to ask questions right away. And having a lawyer's turn of mind, he became suspicious when his questions weren't answered forthrightly.

"See here, Monica," he said, as they drove along. "Something's happened. What was it?"

It felt so good to be safe at home, so overpoweringly good, Monica thought, after all the fright she had felt during the day, after all the questions that had hounded her—questions like "Suppose I can't find a job?" "Suppose I have to telephone home, and Corky laughs at me, and Aunt Willa thinks I can't be trusted?" Against her present security, all the dread uncertainties of the day crowded in. And weariness weighed her down like bricks.

"Confess, Monica," said Corky, and his voice wasn't mocking, or critical, or even unkind. It was only concerned. "What in the world happened to you?"

Monica started to answer. Gathering up in her mind all the incidents of the day, all the disappointment, all the fright, she prepared to tell Corky everything. Then, suddenly, she burst into crying.

"Oh, darn it!" she stamped her foot. "It's stupid to cry!"

"Monicky lost her money, Corky," reported Benny.

"Lost your money, Monica?"

Monica's head, lowered into a handkerchief, nodded.

"She lost her money, and couldn't buy our circus tickets," said Doak.

"But you saw the circus, didn't you?" asked Corky.

"Uh-uh," said Doak, shaking his head.

"You didn't even see the circus? Why—"

"She lost our bus tickets home, too," reported Benny.

A puzzled expression came into Corky's face.

"Jeepers! How in the world did you get home?" he asked.

"Monica earned the money. Didn't you, Monica?" said Doak.

"She ironed a woman's clothes, and the woman paid her money," explained Benny.

"And she got jobs for us, too," added Doak. "We earned enough to buy our pigeons. Tomorrow we're going to get them."

"Why, Monica!"

Amazement, and concern, and admiration—all spilled together out of Corky's voice. "Why didn't you telephone home, Monica?" he asked. "A policeman would have loaned you a dime to call long distance. You know one of the hired men could have helped Harlan and I could have come for you."

For a moment longer Monica sobbed into her handkerchief until all her fright was gone and she felt washed clean. Then, taking a deep breath, she wiped her eyes. She blew her nose. She laughed.

"There's nothing like a good cry to make you feel fresh as a daisy," she declared. "We didn't phone you because we didn't need to phone you. We got home, didn't we?"

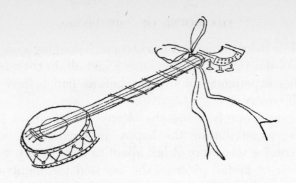

CHAPTER EIGHT

Swing Like Thunder

The following morning, Monica, Doak, and Benny, riding Firefly, set out to buy the pigeons. Monica was in the saddle. Benny, directly behind, was sandwiched between her and Doak. In one hand, Doak held a small wooden crate in which to carry home the fantails, and with the other he slapped Firefly's rump now and then to coax her into a trot.

"How do you boys feel after our excursion yesterday?" asked Monica as they passed the mailbox at the end of the lane, and she turned Firefly west on the graveled road.

"I feel plumb good," answered Doak, emphatically.

"I feel plumb good, too," echoed Benny, just as emphatically.

"Let's make it unanimous," suggested Monica. "I feel plumb good, too." Well, she thought, her legs still ached from standing most of yesterday, and she was still trying to wake up. But how good, how wonderfully good, it felt after yesterday to be safe!

129

And to belong. She had a feeling of belonging now in the house of the Fifers. The Fifers, one and all, in their concern over her experiences of the day before, had helped her to that discovery.

Jogging leisurely along the sleepy country road toward the river, and sharing the happy anticipation of her two small cousins who were at last about to come into possession of a pair of fantail pigeons, she assessed the merits of her discovery. It was good, she sensed, to belong—plumb good.

As she listened to the chatter behind her, she noted with relief that there seemed to be no harbored resentment on the part of Doak and Benny that they had not seen the circus. Nor did they seem to be aware of the heat, although Benny, she thought, must be very warm indeed, scrouged between her and Doak as he was; nor of the drought, although its imprint was everywhere about them.

Monica recalled that one day, summers ago, she and Nancy had ridden Firefly on that same road that for a distance of two miles wound high along a ridge of hills, and then dipped abruptly to the river. That day cardinals and robins sang from sweet-gum thickets, dickcissels whistled from telephone wires, and red-winged blackbirds swayed on cattails growing in a moist ditch beside the road. Now she listened in vain for birdsong. The birds had gone elsewhere for seed and beetle and grub where Nature was less harsh.

A dry rustling among the branches of a locust tree beside the road caused Monica to look up. A gust of hot wind spilled dead twisted leaves on her upturned face. The whole tree, she saw, was dead of thirst. So were its relatives, the other locusts, and its companions and neighbors, the sweet gums and the sour gums, and even the maples. A hay rake stood idle in a nearby field, and, in another, dry blades rustled on spindly cornstalks that were scarcely knee high. And everywhere, as far as the eye could reach into the hollows and across the rolling meadows, the earth was brown, and baked, and parched with thirst, and very tired. And still the sun beat on it and showed no mercy.

From the highest point on the ridge road the valley of the broad Ohio came suddenly into view. Ordinarily the river was muddy from topsoil washed into it by rains along its course. Now it lay docile within its banks, low in its bed, and blue and clear.

The drought, reflected Monica, was more than met the eye. It was more than baked fields and trees dead of thirst, and spindly corn with no sweet nourishment in it. It was an influence reaching into the lives of the people who lived in the farmhouses along the way, ordering a hard, lean winter ahead for them, and hard toil in rebuilding pastures, and herds, and bank accounts. It was putting them in debt. It was slimming down their chances of college.

"I'll tell you how to get there, Monica," Doak interrupted her thoughts. "You stay right on this road till you come almost to the river. Then you take a dirt road that runs off to the left. I'll show you when you get there."

"The boy with the pigeons lives down there," added Benny.

"Sure thing," said Monica. She kicked Firefly in the ribs to urge her on a little faster. "We're almost there."

"Shucks, man!" sighed Doak. "When we get those pigeons—"

The owner of the pigeons, a boy of about fifteen, led the way to the barn. "Thought you two wasn't a comin'," he said.

"You—you haven't sold 'em all, have you?" Doak asked haltingly.

"Naw. Got two left to sell. Jest two. A male and a female."

He slid back the wooden latch of the door to a stall that had been boarded up for the pigeons, opened the door a crack, and stepped inside. Then, cautiously, he held the door just wide enough for the others to enter, one at a time.

Inside the dim, musty stall, Monica blinked her eyes and stared in amazement at the two pigeons perched on a dark corner roost—two dazzlingly white birds, their gleaming necks arched backward until their haughty heads rested against their fanlike tails.

"Boys!" she gasped. "Why didn't you tell me they were like that?"

"We did tell you," Doak said.

"But you didn't tell me they looked like the North Pole," said Monica. "And so proud! They're icy, they're so proud!"

"Yeah, so they are," the owner agreed as he moved quietly toward the roost. "That struttin' stuff comes natural to 'em. They keep their distance."

He caught the birds firmly by their shoulders, and, as they uttered querulous little complaints, he put them into the crate Doak had brought.

"You want to take good care of 'em now, fellers," he said. "I won't have no more to sell till next year."

They started back to Firefly, Doak and Benny in front, speechless with accomplishment, carrying the crate between them.

"You want to feed 'em lots of grit along with their grain," the boy instructed. He took the crate and held it until the three of them mounted Firefly. Then he handed it up to Doak.

"Shucks, man!" Doak assured him. "We'll feed 'em grit, all right."

"Bushels of it," said Benny.

Homeward they jogged along the ridge road, Doak and Benny making clucking, purring noises in their throats—"pigeon language," Benny explained—and counting their baby pigeons in flocks before so much as an egg was laid. The completeness of their joy was infectious, spreading to Monica, who began to feel that missing the circus had had its rewards. They were all the gainers, even she, who had almost won Corky's respect.

"What are you going to name your pigeons?" she asked. "They ought to have fancy names, don't you think? No ordinary names for these extraordinary creatures!"

"You like 'em, Monicky?" asked Benny.

"Um-*hum!*" said Monica.

"We could name the female Snow White," suggested Benny.

"What would we name the male then?" asked Doak. "I think Queenie'd be a good name for the female. And King for the male."

Monica smiled to herself. Doak was always the practical one, going straight to the heart of matters. Benny was the one with poetry in him. Plain and Fancy, Uncle Steve had called them. She felt a great affection for them both, but it was Benny she understood, Benny whose self put forth timid tendrils and wound them around her.

"Instead of naming her Queenie," she suggested, "how would you like to name her for a queen who was beautiful and proud?"

"Suits me," agreed Doak.

"Suits the pigeon, too," said Benny. " 'Beautiful and proud.' What was the queen's name?"

"Guinevere."

"That's a kind of funny name," said Doak.

"But not everybody has a name as proud as that," Benny told him. "It just suits our pigeon, I think."

"Guinevere was loved by a proud and handsome knight," Monica told them. "Too proud and handsome for his own good. Named Sir Lancelot du Lac. Do you like that name for the male?"

"Did he wear a coat of mail?" asked Benny. "Like I saw in a museum one time?"

"Yes. And he rode a beautiful charger."

"Sir Lancelot du Lac and Guinevere. Sir Lancelot du Lac and Guinevere," repeated Benny, getting his ear used to the proud names.

"We can call 'em Lance and Gwen for short," announced Doak.

Benny, wedged between Monica and Doak, craned his neck to see the pigeons huddled in a corner of the small crate.

"Isn't Guinevere proud?" he mused.

"Yep," agreed Doak. "So's Lance."

Nancy was waiting at the gate as they came jogging over the hill and past the barn. As they neared the house she began to laugh. It was the first time Monica had heard her laugh since T-Bone was sold.

"Do you know what you look like?" Nancy called. "Like the outfit that made the princess laugh till she coughed up the fishbone."

"You wait till you see what we've got," Doak told her. "Here," he handed the crate to her. "You can hold 'em while we get down. Don't scare 'em, Nancy. Man, you got to be gentle with these things."

Nancy took the crate, and, while the three dismounted, she thrust a finger between the bars, rubbed the gleaming feathers of the pigeons, and admired their dazzling whiteness.

"They almost put your eyes out," she said.

"Man, they sure do!" agreed Doak. "Come on, Benny," he took the crate from Nancy and started toward a small deserted henhouse that they had prepared for the pigeons. "We got to put this king and queen in their castle," Benny explained to Nancy. "And give 'em their banquet."

"We got to put 'em in the old henhouse and feed 'em grit," amended Doak.

Nancy was still waiting at the gate when Monica returned from the barn where she had taken Firefly. "How'd you like to go to a square dance?" she asked.

"A square dance?" repeated Monica, her face lighting. "When? Where?"

"Next Friday night. In Colgate High gym," Nancy told her. "We 4-H-ers have planned it. To celebrate the drought."

Monica considered the information. "How are you going?" she asked.

"With George," said Nancy. "He'll be home that week end. I had a letter this morning."

"Do I have to have a date?" asked Monica.

"Of course not," Nancy assured her. "Most girls come with dates. But some fellows will be there without dates."

For a moment Monica toyed with the prospect. She had learned square dancing in gym classes at home, and sometimes Mimi's crowd had square danced. Monica loved the swing and the rapid movement of the dances. To go bowing

to corners, and swinging with partners, and weaving grace-
fully around a circle in the allemande after all these anxious
weeks of drought and drudgery seemed an exquisite sort of
prospect.

"I could get a date for you," she heard Nancy offering.

"Well—" Monica hesitated, fearful that Nancy's choice for
her might turn out to be of the apron-stitching variety.
"Maybe a date isn't necessary if there'll be some footloose
males around," she said. "Are they good dancers?"

"They're not bad," said Nancy. "Some of them have put
on exhibition dances at the State Fair."

"Really?" Monica busied herself with her thoughts. It
hadn't occurred to her before to date anybody in Colgate. She
hastily shoved into the background the idea she had brought
from home that Colgate boys weren't quite her type—and
Mimi's.

"How would I get there if I didn't have a date?" she asked.

"George and I can take you, of course," said Nancy.

"You're sure three isn't a crowd?"

"Silly!" scolded Nancy. "Corky may want to go with us,
too," she added. "His girl's out of town for a couple of weeks.
And I'm sure Harlan and Coralie are going."

"What'll I wear?" asked Monica.

"Anything," said Nancy. "Just any dress. It doesn't matter."

"But you have that square dance dress you modeled at the
show," objected Monica. "A dress like that makes you feel
so much more—more festive. And," she added knowingly,
"something tells me this is going to be festive!"

"Monica!" exclaimed Nancy. "I almost didn't ask you to
go. I didn't think you'd want to."

"I guess I wouldn't have, earlier," admitted Monica. "Three
or four weeks ago."

They started up the maple-shaded walk toward the house.

"I have an idea," said Nancy. "I'll make you a square-dance dress."

In the fragment of a second that Monica looked at her cousin, she realized she had stumbled on to another discovery. Nancy's actions that had often seemed rankly officious were something else entirely. They were part of Nancy's energetic self; she couldn't help being generous any more than she could help being pretty and petite and sparkling. The rare, heaped-up measure of her generosity was the thing that had annoyed Monica—that, and Monica's own desire to find faults.

"Oh, Nancy, would you?" she asked. "One like yours?"

The conversation at the dinner table was centered on Lancelot and Guinevere, and, whenever it strayed in any direction, it was promptly headed off by Doak and Benny, and brought back to center. Much of their talk consisted of sighs, and worshipful exclamations of wonder, and from their conversation it was evident they planned to spend the afternoon—if not the rest of the summer—in the vicinity of the pigeons' castle.

While the table talk was centered on pigeons, Monica was free to think of other, more private, matters. She was thinking that she hadn't wholly earned Corky's respect. She hadn't produced a performance that could wholly silence what Aunt Willa called his "free speech." Certainly he recognized she was trying to redeem herself when she stayed home from Morganfield to cook a hot meal. Her intentions rated high in that instance, even Corky had admitted, but her performance was far from passable. Certain it was, too, that he admired her for earning her way home from Evansville un-

aided. But how could he think it other than childish careless-
ness that she had lost her wallet?

"Nancy," she said as they were clearing the table after
lunch, "do you suppose I could make my square-dance dress
myself?"

"Why don't you want me to make it?" asked Nancy.

"It isn't that I don't want you to make it," Monica explained thoughtfully. "It's just that—that—well, I don't think
I can make you understand because you don't know what it's
like not to know how to do things. Not to know how to do
anything at all."

"What do you mean, you don't know how to do anything?" Nancy asked.

Monica slumped down on the kitchen stool. "When you
have a housekeeper instead of a mother, Nancy," she said,
looking hard at the floor and trying to find her way through
her thoughts, "you—you miss a lot of things. One thing you
think you're glad you're missing is work—chores—washing
dishes, and ironing, and cleaning your room, and all that.
But, of course, what you're really missing is learning how to
do things that'll make other people respect you."

"Don't be silly!" Nancy told her. "I respect you without
your knowing how to make a square-dance dress."

"But you'd respect me more if I did. And I'd respect myself," said Monica. "Don't you see?"

Monica's voice was taut, begging for understanding. In
the brief silence that followed she wondered if one person
could ever genuinely understand another. Or was every person wrapped up in her own little world like a cocoon, so
tight that no one else could enter?

"Well, of course, Monica," she heard Nancy saying, "if
you want to make it yourself, you can. You've got a whole

week, and it's easy to learn to sew. I'll show you how—if you want me to."

"Oh, Nancy, would you?" she begged, grateful that, although Nancy scarcely understood her need for making the dress, she accepted her reasons on good faith. "Do you suppose Aunt Willa would drive to town with us this afternoon to get the material?"

"And a pattern," added Nancy. "It's easier when you have a pattern."

Aunt Willa listened with delight to their plans. Uncle Steve would go to town with them, too, she said. A drive would do him good. He could sit in the car while they shopped. They would be ready as soon as she could change her dress.

"Oh!" Monica put her hand to her face in a gesture of remembering. "I haven't any money to buy material. I took all my money to the circus, and lost it."

"You get your allowance soon, don't you?" asked Nancy.

Monica calculated. "Not for two weeks," she said. "Not till toward the end of July."

"Let's forget the allowance," said Aunt Willa. "I want to give you the material, Monica, as a thank-you for using your head so well in Evansville."

As they drove along the highway into Colgate, Monica felt happier than at any time during the summer. Maybe, she thought to herself, she was happier than at any time during her life. Silently she counted her summer's accomplishments. She had learned to milk a cow. She had learned to drive a car. She had learned to iron. Why, she could make her living at ironing, if she had to. Now she was going to learn to sew. And, added to all that, she had made a place for herself among the Fifers.

Well, she amended her thinking, among most of the Fifers. She couldn't rid herself of the lurking suspicion that Corky still had reservations about her. Corky wanted some convincing still that she had a claim to his whole-hearted respect, with no reservations, no strings attached, as Nancy had.

They left Uncle Steve waiting in the car and chatting with passers-by while they went in search of material. Monica had anticipated buying material like Nancy's. But she lost her heart instead to pastel shades, in particular to soft blue cotton, sprigged with pink moss roses. But the picture she glimpsed of herself sashaying and do-ci-doing in such flattering finery was blurred by her suspicion that not merely by making the dress would she quite have won the respect of Corky. Not yet would she have made him eat his words, clean, with not a crumb left.

"This material will make up into a lovely dress," she heard Aunt Willa saying. "And the color is just perfect for you, Monica." Aunt Willa could see no reason for dilly-dallying.

"Aunt Willa," Monica said, after long moments of fingering the material, of trying to get her thoughts to run in straight channels rather than in circles, and of attempting to say what she was believing she ought to say, "maybe I won't get the material this afternoon, after all."

Aunt Willa and Nancy stared at her. "But, why?" they asked.

"Well," she hesitated, "I'm just not sure about it."

"Don't you like this, Monica?" asked Nancy. "It was just made for you."

"Sure," said Monica. "I like it."

"Do you want to look at material in another store?" asked
Aunt Willa.

"No," said Monica. "I couldn't find anything I like better
than this."

"Then what are we waiting for?" Aunt Willa wanted to
know.

"It'll take some time to make the dress," Nancy reminded
her. "You ought to get your material this afternoon so you'll
have plenty of time for it."

"If I get it Monday, I can make it, can't I?" asked Monica.

"Oh, yes, sure," said Nancy.

"Then I'll wait till Monday to decide."

"Why, Monica—"

Nonplussed, Aunt Willa and Nancy followed her out of
the store and down the street, past the variety store, past
the drug store, and the bank and the hardware store, past
the drive-in restaurant with a "Girl Wanted" sign in the
window, across the railroad tracks to the car. They wondered,
and they hinted for explanations. But explanations from
Monica were not forthcoming. She had decided not to get
the material, she said. That was all there was to it.

The next morning, as soon as the chores were finished,
Monica asked, "May I borrow your bike this morning,
Nancy?"

"Sure," said Nancy. "Where you going?"

"Oh," Monica evaded her, "nowhere much."

"When are you coming back?"

"After a while."

"Monica, what's the matter with you?" Nancy demanded.

"Is anything the matter with me?" asked Monica.

"You're acting so queer," said Nancy. "As if you're keeping
something from us."

"Am I?" asked Monica. And she went in search of Aunt Willa.

"If you haven't something you want me to do this morning, Aunt Willa," she said. "I'd like to go to town. I'm going to ride Nancy's bike."

Aunt Willa was brushing off Bridget's Porch. She leaned her broom against the wall and looked solicitously at Monica.

"What's the matter, Monica?" she asked.

"Not a thing," Monica assured her.

"Do you need to go into town?"

"Yes, Aunt Willa."

"If you wait a while, I can go with you in the car."

"I can go alone, Aunt Willa."

Aunt Willa turned away and picked up her broom, looked at Monica again, and began sweeping.

"All right," she said. "When will you be home?"

"If I'm not home at noon, I'll call you," Monica promised.

It was a hot trip into town with the sun beating down on her. She hadn't been on a bike all summer, and her legs grew tired from pedaling up the hills. The miles seemed unusually long.

She parked the bike in front of the drive-in restaurant and went inside. A few latecomers were eating their breakfasts in the booths. A bald-headed little man wearing nose glasses was waiting on them. He was wrapped, cocoonlike, in a long white apron, and he walked briskly between the booths and the counter on which a fat Negro woman was slamming plates of bacon and scrambled eggs and toast. He looked down his thin nose as he spoke to his customers.

On one of his return trips to the counter, he took time to notice Monica, who had remained standing near the door.

"You want breakfast, Miss?" he asked. "Take that booth over in the corner."

"Are you the manager?" Monica asked, keeping her voice low.

"I'm the owner." The man scowled. "What did you want?"

"I saw your ad in the window," Monica told him. "The ad that says 'Girl Wanted.' I came to apply."

"It's a night job," said the man. "Waiting on the drive-in customers from five to ten."

"Oh," said Monica, "I don't believe I can work nights. I live in the country. I couldn't get home."

"Then I can't give you a job," he said. And leaving her, he deftly filled two cups with coffee and carried them to a table.

"Unless," he said as he passed her again, "you want to wash dishes for a couple of days. My dishwasher got down with the heat yesterday. She ought to be back by day after tomorrow."

Monica hesitated. The smells that came from the kitchen were close and stuffy. Maybe the dishwasher had reason for getting down with the heat.

"Well," barked the man, "take it or leave it."

"I'd have to get home before dark," said Monica.

"You can get off at sundown."

"What will you pay me?"

"Thirty an hour," said the man. "For inexperienced help like you."

Two days at thirty cents an hour, calculated Monica, would be more than enough to buy the material for the dress.

"I can start now," she said.

He marched before her into the smelly, hot kitchen heated by an ancient, black, coal-burning stove. Dirty dishes were piled in mounds in a dirty sink. Nothing was in order. It was the sort of kitchen to throw a good housekeeper into a dither until she set it straight. It was not love of housekeeping, however, but visions of herself twirling in a lovely square-dance frock that sustained Monica as she pitched into the mess.

At noon Monica phoned Aunt Willa and told her the story. She half expected a scolding, but Aunt Willa only said, "I suspected something like that, child. You didn't need to punish yourself so hard for losing your money."

At the supper table that night, Monica could only remark to herself how things had changed since the first evening she ate dinner with the Fifers. Then she had felt shut out of their conversation. Now they wanted her to do all the talking—to describe with variations her reactions to the mound of dirty dishes, how the cook managed to keep the owner afraid of her tongue, how the drive-in girls imitated Old Pinch Penny, as they called the owner. But she was glad the dishwasher was improved. One more day of washing dirty dishes in that kitchen was enough for a lifetime, she calculated.

On Monday morning, Monica, carefully guarding her well-earned money, drove to town once more with Nancy and Aunt Willa, and, without a moment's debate, bought the material and a pattern. At home, Nancy painstakingly interpreted the pattern language to her, helped her cut the dress, and stood by to supervise the sewing.

Lowering the sewing-machine needle into the material and running the first seam was to Monica as exciting as anything she had done all summer. She laughed merrily above the whir of the motor as she watched the lengthening seam.

"It's not quite fair!" she laughed. "The machine does most of it!"

Seam by seam the skirt took shape under Monica's fingers,

and, after the skirt, the blouse with its round low neck and
its dainty cap sleeves. Not once did her enthusiasm wane,
not even when Nancy recommended that puckered seams
be taken out and done over.

When the dress was finished and pressed, and hung up to
wait for Friday night, Monica felt foolishly happy and
secure. Strangely, however, she no longer was concerned
about what Corky might be thinking about her. Maybe, she
thought, it was for herself all along that she had been trying
to win her self-respect. And now she had it, completely,
perfectly.

On Friday night as she stood in her new frock, turning
herself before the long mirror in the front hall, Doak, followed by Benny, came in from the pigeons' castle where they
had been taking a last look for the night at Lancelot and
Guinevere. Her freshly shampooed hair, swept up from her
ears and neck, held soft glints from the light. Her throat was
smooth and firm, her shoulders straight above the curving
neck of the dress, her blue eyes were bright with excitement.

"Um-m-m!" said Doak, pausing to look at her. "Pretty!"

"Humph!" snorted Benny, hurrying kitchenward. "Always
was!"

Then George came, and he and Nancy, Corky and Monica
were off to the dance.

"Don't be silly!" Monica scolded herself over and over as
they drove into town. "This is just a square dance. Nothing
but a square dance, with country boys and girls who've lost
everything they had in the drought. And you're feeling like
a royal princess going to a royal ball."

But self-scolding had no effect on her. She was ridiculously
happy, and she liked being that way. And nothing, she felt,
could happen to her to mar the evening.

Nothing did. The fiddlers tuned up, the caller mounted the platform.

All into your places, brighten up your faces,
Tighten up your traces for a good long haul!

"All right, everybody. Let's start off with the Grand March. Corky Fifer, hunt you up a partner and lead off. Everybody follow."

Tighten your belt, pull down your vest,
Swing with the gal that you love best.

"Monica," Corky said, at her elbow, "will you lead off with me?"

They took their places at the head of the line, and the other couples fell in behind them. The music began. Along the wall on each side, the couples promenaded to the foot of the long gym, turned to the center, and marched down the center to the head of the gym. There they turned to the right and left, promenaded again to the foot of the gym, and back again to the head in fours. Then the fours promenaded, and back again to the head in eights, and the eights promenaded back in sixteens. Then began the serpentine, with Monica in the lead, weaving the lengthening line to the marching music in and out of the formations until she stood in the center, and then weaving counterclockwise until she was once more at the end.

"Swing Like Thunder," announced the caller.

At once the couples formed their squares.

First couple out to the couple on the right,
Circle four for half the night.

The caller kept up an incessant patter.

Hands across!
Ladies bow!
Gents bow under!
Hold your holts and swing like thunder!

With right feet forward, the four dancers, forming an interlocking basket, whirled giddily around.

Drop your hands and circle four,
Leave that couple and pass right o'er,
On to the next.

Gaily dancing, Monica and Corky, the head couple, passed on to the third couple in their square.

Allemande left to the corner you go,
Grand chain eight around the row,
Wave the ocean, wave the sea,
Wave that pretty gal back to me, and promenade!

No sooner had they finished swinging like thunder when away they went again, through Birdie in the Cage, through the Turkey Wing, through the boisterous Grapevine Twist, through the swaying, swinging Texas Star, through the Double Sashay, through the Wagon Wheel.

It was past midnight when Nancy, Monica, and Corky trooped through the house to the kitchen to raid the refrigerator, and then up the stairs to their bedrooms.

"Oh, my feet!" groaned Nancy, as she flopped into one of the wing chairs and let her shoes drop to the floor.

"I'll groan about my feet tomorrow," said Monica as she brushed her hair before the mirror. "Tonight I don't feel my feet. I'm still floating on air."

Gathering up the edges of her skirt, she twirled around and around in the middle of the floor.

"Say!" she said, stopping suddenly in front of the portrait over the mantel. "Wonder what Great-aunt Eugenia would have thought about tonight?"

"I imagine," said Nancy, "she would have thought nobody in all the world—but nobody!—ever had had such a good time as you were having."

"And she would have been right!" declared Monica. "Absolutely right!"

And gathering up her skirt, she began to twirl again.

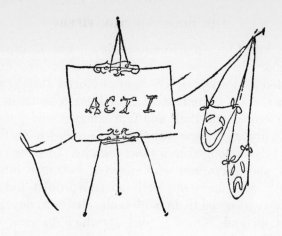

CHAPTER NINE

Shakespeare & Company

Darkness was just beginning to lift from the earth the next morning when Monica found herself awake. In the fragile light she could see the leaves on the maple trees extended motionless from the branches, and, in the branches she could hear the cicadas tuning up for another hot day.

She wondered why she had awakened so early when Nancy was still sound asleep. The excitement she had felt the evening before seemed to have hovered over her in the night, and now to stand waiting to go with her through the day, even on such humdrum errands as the milking.

Why, she wondered, should she have been so excited about the square dancing? She had danced just as giddily at Mimi's parties. Mimi? Why did Mimi seem so many thousands of miles away, she wondered, so out of the present picture?

Why did Mimi seem so out of the picture of the days to come, too?

Startled by the discovery, Monica looked ahead to school days in the fall. Mimi, she realized for a certainty—Mimi and her crowd and their constant comings and goings and buzzings about, and the way they gave their lessons the once over lightly—belonged to a time gone by. To school days in the fall, she discovered with surprise, belonged other girls and boys—girls and boys with no convertibles but only a jalopy or two among them, with home chores to do, and with after-school and Saturday jobs at which to earn a little money. These, she realized, she was akin to now by reason of her summer in the house of the Fifers—by reason of Aunt Willa's insistence that blue jeans be ironed as slick as a mirror, of Uncle Steve's knowing that, in spite of drought and disaster, God is here and now, of Corky's needling her into picking up her share of the load and, like everybody else, carrying it along willingly.

The thought of school days in the fall brought her father to mind. She felt anxious to be at home again, to take up their life where they had left it off, not last spring, but springs ago when they had been companions in work and play, when he had enjoyed her friends, and had been to her what Uncle Steve had been this summer. In five more weeks she would be going home. They would be pleasant weeks, she sensed, during which, now that the great sacrifice had been made to the drought, life would follow the more rhythmic pattern of the Roller Coaster Road—first up on little peaks, and then down in little hollows.

Nancy stirred, turned in bed, and settled again.

Maybe it was selfish, thought Monica, to have enjoyed the square dancing with such reckless happiness when the others were dancing to forget the drought, and their projects baked in fields and gardens, and their plans charred by the unrelenting sun. It was true, as Nancy had said, that she had never gone without anything. Because she had never watched helplessly while a dream blew away on a hot, burning wind, a barrier stood between her and the others, between her and Nancy. And whether or not the barrier had a gateway through which she could pass, she didn't know.

Nancy stirred again.

"You awake?" Monica whispered.

Nancy did not answer.

Quietly Monica slid out of bed and pulled on her blue jeans and shirt.

"What you doing?" yawned Nancy.

"Going to milk," said Monica.

"Um-m-m!" groaned Nancy, and slept again.

Gathering milk pails from Bridget's Porch, Monica started to the barn. She was well past the cottonwood when she heard Corky call to her cautiously from his west bedroom window. "Hey, Monicky! Wait up!"

She set her pails down among the crotchety roots of the cottonwood. While she waited, she watched the sun boiling up red in the glassy sky, full of distress and disaster. Aunt Willa's chickens came flocking to her in a white trainlike procession in the hope of being fed. But finding nothing scattered from her hand, they turned away to cast beady eyes on the hard-baked earth, or to scratch fruitlessly among the parched weeds and grasses.

"Where's your girl friend?" asked Corky, joining her.

"Asleep," said Monica. "I'm going to milk for her this morning."

Corky took the milk pails from her.

"I can help you," he said. "Harlan and I are going to build silos this morning, but we've got plenty of time. In fact, we've got almost nothing to do for a month but build two silos and fill them."

He opened the barnyard gate and let her pass through. The cattle had trooped down from the hillside pasture and were huddled back of the barnyard bawling for their breakfast.

"Why don't you feed them their cornstalks?" asked Monica. "I can milk. If I'm not through by the time you are, you can help me."

"Good enough," he agreed, and he climbed into the truck and started for the cornfield.

Monica watched him as he drove out of the barnyard. Corky, she realized, had needled her for the last time. She had no longer need to be on guard against his barbs. He had shot his last barb. They were equals now. They could be natural, and frank, and free.

There were still two of the cows to be milked when Corky had finished feeding the other cattle.

"Know what?" asked Corky as he squatted beside one of the cows and began milking her while Monica milked the other.

"What?" asked Monica.

"Got an idea," he announced. "There'll be dances at Princeton this fall. If Uncle Abbott'll let you come down some time, I'll get a date for you with a nice fellow."

Monica stopped milking and peered around the cow at him.

"You mean that, Corky?" she asked.

"Sure!" he said. "There're chaperones and things like that. Tell you what. I'll write Uncle Abbott myself and ask him."

Monica resumed her milking.

"Daddy wouldn't have let me go last year," she mused, remembering the grief she had caused him. "But this year I think, maybe, he'll feel differently about it. And whenever you have a free week end, Corky, you could come up and spend it with us."

"I'd already planned to come up Thanksgiving," he said.

"Good!" she said. "I'll tell Daddy."

There was silence between them for a few seconds as the milk rose in their pails.

"I wish Nancy could be there, too," said Monica. "It's kind of like leaving her out of good times."

"Nancy'll be having her own good times," Corky assured her. "Don't worry about Nancy."

"But she clammed up so for a while," complained Monica.

"That was to be expected," said Corky. "When you're hit hard on the head, it takes a little while to get over being stunned."

"Will she really have to give up college, Corky?"

"Not Nancy!" he said. "Nancy won't have to give up entirely anything she wants. If the main road's blocked off, she'll find a detour. But it takes time. And a lot of thinking. And a lot of work. Nancy's quite a gal."

A car, trailed by a thick cloud of yellow dust, rolled into the barnyard.

"I'm still dizzy from swinging like thunder," Harlan said as he climbed out. "Monica, why you been keeping from us all summer how you can dance?"

"Nobody asked me to a dance before," Monica teased him.

"You ought to stay all winter and go to school with Nancy," he said. "We have square dances almost every Saturday night."

"We have 'em, too," said Monica. "But for some reason or other, I never had so much fun dancing in my life as I had last night."

"Soon's you finish breakfast, Corky," Harlan changed the subject, "we'll get busy on the silos."

"Do you know that the last pond in the west pasture is about dry, Harlan?" asked Corky. "I looked at it yesterday."

"That makes six of the seven dry," said Harlan, his voice subdued. "From now until rain—until a week of soaking rains—we'll have to haul water to the stock from the pump here at the barn. I might as well put Cowboy Mullins on that job and plan nothing else for him to do."

On the way to the house from the milking, Monica scanned the sky for some sign of a break in the drought.

"It may be October before they get rain," prophesied Corky as he noticed her occupation. "Or even winter."

"What'll they do?" asked Monica.

"They'll have to make out any way they can," said Corky. "It's one thing when you can run away from disaster the way you and I can. You and I and Benny. It's something else to stand and wait till rain makes the world over."

A couple of mornings later, after Harlan and Corky had fashioned two huge, two-tiered circles of snow fence in the cornfield across the driveway from the house, and lined them with tar paper, they drove the truck into the cornfield and set to work cutting the cornstalks.

Monica sat under the maples with Uncle Steve and watched them whack away at the earless cornstalks and throw them into the truck.

"They cover as much ground filling the truck with cornstalks this year," said Uncle Steve, "as they covered last year gathering a truck load of corn."

Uncle Steve was restless. After watching a while, he took up his crutches and hobbled to the Kinfolks Porch. But hardly was he seated when he pulled himself up a second time and went into the house, as if he couldn't quite bear to watch this eldest child of his salvage such meager stores from his defeat.

Watching him, Monica sensed more keenly than ever that though Harlan and Nancy—all the Fifers living on the farm —were giving up much, she was giving up nothing, suffering nothing, wanting nothing, changing no plans because the sun and the hot winds had baked the Fifer farm. Instead, she was looking ahead confidently and happily to the future.

Twenty-five acres of stunted, earless cornstalks Harlan and Corky cut and packed into the squat silos, and sealed over with tar paper. When that was done, Corky announced that he might as well be going home. The ground couldn't be plowed, and Balbo rye couldn't be sowed for fall pastures until rain fell, and, until then, Harlan and Cowboy Mullins had little to do but keep the stock watered.

The next day, while Monica and Nancy sat cross-legged on the floor of Corky's room, watching him pack, they speculated with him concerning his first year at Princeton, and vowed to vote for him when he ran for President of the United States.

"Jumping Jeepers, Nancy!" Corky exclaimed suddenly, as he stopped in his packing and scratched his head. "Know what I've found? A present Mom sent you back in June."

From the bottom of his trunk he took a small white box and handed it to Nancy. "What'll Mom think of me?" he speculated.

"What'll she think of me?" asked Nancy as she tore away the tissue wrappings. From out of the box she lifted a silver bracelet, two narrow bands connected with a lattice work of silver flowers.

"Corky!" she scolded. "If you hadn't been so forgetful, I could have worn this to the square dance last night."

"Sorry!" said Corky. "But something tells me there'll be other square dances in your life."

"I'll run write Aunt Ruth right away," said Nancy, hurrying out of the room.

"While I'm passing out presents," Corky said, turning to Monica, "here's a good-by present for you." He handed her a sealed envelope.

Curiously, Monica tore open the envelope. In it she found a short length of blue ribbon, a couple of inches wide, cut straight across the top and with an indented V at the bottom, after the manner of prize ribbons. On it was lettered in bold, black pencil,

The
Summer
of the
Drought

*   *   *

First Place

"Well," she held the ribbon up, laughing, "what's the significance of this? What do I get a blue ribbon for?"

"Because I thought you'd earned it, Monicky," said Corky. "That night you came home from the circus, I decided to give you this. You sure came through this summer."

Mist covered Monica's eyes as she stared at the ribbon. "Thanks, Corky," she managed to say. "Thanks a lot."

She got up from the floor and started to her room. At the doorway she turned. "I don't really deserve it, Corky,"

she said, "but thanks, anyway. I'll try to stay within holler-
ing distance of—of the thing you think it stands for."

That evening Harlan and Coralie came for supper, as
festive a supper as Aunt Willa could concoct out of a grocery
store. After the dishes were washed, the Fifers sat on the
Kinfolks Porch, and, as a big moon came up out of the east
and covered the parched earth with a kinder light than that
from the sun, they talked about the summer. It was a time
for recalling Monica's first lesson in milking, the 4-H style
show at which she had modeled Mike's apron, and the pork
chops that rattled on the plates like chips of wood—all amus-
ing things to remember now.

When Doak began to yawn, and Benny, sitting in the swing
beside Aunt Willa, leaned his head against her shoulder,
Uncle Steve got to his crutches and went into the living
room. Quietly the others followed.

Opening the Bible, he read:

To everything there is a season,
And a time to every purpose under heaven:
A time to be born, and a time to die;
A time to plant, and a time to pluck up that which is
    planted. . . .
I have seen the travail
Which God hath given to the sons of men to be exercised
    in it.
He hath made everything beautiful in his time.

When Corky had gone, the house of the Fifers was
strangely quiet. All activity, save the ordinary, everyday
chores, seemed suspended. Monica began to feel that life
would never rise to a roller-coaster peak as she had imagined it would.

Then, one day, the phone rang.

"George?" Monica whispered after listening a moment to Nancy's conversation.

Nancy nodded.

"Just a minute. I'll see," Nancy said into the transmitter. She turned to Monica.

"Want a date? To go swimming?" she asked.

"With whom?" Monica whispered, excited.

Nancy cupped her hand over the transmitter.

"George's cousin, Bob Brent," she explained. "They want us to go to Marion with them. To the swimming pool there."

"What's he like?" whispered Monica.

"Lots of fun," said Nancy. "Lives in Paducah. Senior. Basketball team. Black hair. Good looking."

"I'll take him," whispered Monica.

All afternoon, Monica and Bob, George and Nancy dived and swam and played in the cool water. If she hadn't been so wretched, if she hadn't behaved like a spoiled brat the first part of the summer, thought Monica, she could have been having fun like this all along.

They reached home at sundown. After George and his cousin had gone, Nancy and Monica hurried to get into their milking clothes. Monica, from the bedroom window, watched Doak and Benny trudge to the old henhouse carrying grit, mash, and water to their pigeons. A minute later, she saw them returning, still carrying the grit, the mash, and the water.

At the edge of the yard, Benny paused and looked toward the house. Then, suddenly he burst into loud, anguished wails. Doak, startled, looked at Benny. Then he, too, burst into wails, pitched slightly lower, but as full of anguish.

"What's the matter, boys?" called Monica.

Without waiting for an answer, she ran down the stairs. On Bridget's Porch she met the boys coming in.

"They're gone," Benny sobbed.

"Lance and Gwen are gone," wailed Doak.

"Gone?" repeated Monica. Her hand went to her throat as she sensed their tragedy. "You must not have looked, boys," she said.

"Yes, we did—did, too," they sobbed.

They set down their buckets and turned their wretched faces pleadingly up to her.

"But the pigeons couldn't get out of the henhouse," she said, still doubting. "How could they have got out?"

"I don't know," sobbed Benny.

"When did you see them last?" asked Monica.

"Just a little while ago," said Doak. "We were down there and—and saw them, sitting on the corner roost where they always sit."

"Did you leave the door open?" asked Monica. "A pigeon can't fly through a wall."

"Maybe—maybe Lancelot and Guinevere could," offered Benny.

Monica looked at the boys a little sternly. "Not even Lancelot and Guinevere could fly through a wall," she said. "Somebody must have left the door open." She put her hand on Benny's shoulder. "Come with me, boys," she said, "and let's look again."

Together they walked to the pigeons' castle, but it was plain to see in one glance that haughtiness in dazzling white no longer lived there.

"You stop crying, boys," Monica tried to console them. "I think we'll find them some place. Let's ask Uncle Steve what he thinks."

"As likely as not, those pigeons have struck right out for the river where they were raised," Uncle Steve told them, "and if you go down there you'll find them sitting on the roost waiting for you."

"But what if they aren't?" sobbed Benny.

"Listen, Uncle Steve," spoke up Monica. "I can do the milking. Why doesn't Nancy drive you and the boys down there right now and see if the pigeons are there?"

Monica had finished milking only one of the cows when the car came in sight over the hill.

"We didn't find them," Nancy called to her as she drove past the barnyard toward the house.

At suppertime the boys shuffled to the table and sat weary, eye-swollen, and heart-broken, with their untouched food before them. No consolation that anyone could offer seemed to reach them, because it did not bring back to them a couple of proud fantail pigeons that had suddenly found a freedom as wide as the world. At last, still sniffling, they begged to go to bed, supperless.

"Shall we read before you go?" asked Uncle Steve. Nancy brought him the Bible, and, opening it, he read:

Then the king commanded, and they brought Daniel, and cast him into the den of lions.

Dutifully the boys sat through the reading, but Daniel and his deliverance from the den of lions seemed far removed from their grievous loss.

"Come on, boys," said Aunt Willa when the reading was finished. "I'll tuck you in tonight. How would you like to sleep in Corky's room?"

In a few moments Monica followed them upstairs, carrying to each of the boys a glass of milk. She sat on their bed while they drank it, and, in an effort to wean them away from their sorrow, she told them about the antics of a dog she had once owned. They listened to her, after a fashion. But she could see they were not listening in their hearts.

In the middle of the night Monica awoke. From Corky's room across the hall came sounds of muffled sobbing. She rose on her elbow and listened.

After a time she slipped out of bed and tiptoed across the hall. Moonlight from the west was flooding the boys' room. Doak, she could see, was sound asleep.

Tiptoeing to the bed, Monica sat down on the edge of it beside Benny, and stroked the damp hair back from his forehead. She wondered what words of comfort she could say to him that would not ring hollow in his ears—she who had not lost a pair of pigeons, who had lost nothing at all.

"Tell me what you're thinking, Benny," she said to him gently.

"I—I'm thinking—about—about—what if something hurts Lancelot and Guinevere," he sobbed.

His words caught at her throat. How was it, she wondered, that so small a boy was crying his heart out not because of his loss of the pigeons, but because of his love of them?

As she sat quietly beside him, she felt herself looking deep into his mind, and discovering there a crystal region filled with gentleness for all living things. Lifting a corner of the sheet, she wiped her eyes.

"Are you—crying, too?" Benny asked.

"Yes," she whispered.

"Do you—know what it's like—to lose some fantail pigeons?"

"Yes, Benny."

"How do you know?"

"Because I love you. And when you are sad because you have lost some pigeons and they may be in danger, then I'm sad, too."

"Hm-m-m!" said Benny. After a moment, he became quiet.

"I've just found that out, Benny," Monica told him. "I didn't know until now that, when you love people, you understand why they're sad, and you're sad with them."

"Hm-m-m!" he said again.

She continued to stroke his forehead. "Would you like me to tell you a story, Benny, to help you go to sleep?"

He snuggled close to her, and made himself comfortable. "Um-hum," he said.

"Let's see," she pondered. *"Goldilocks and the Three Bears?"*

"Uh-uh," he objected.

"The Old Woman and the Little Pig?"

"Uh-uh."

"Jack and the Beanstalk?"

"Don't you know any stories like the stories Uncle Steve reads at bedtime?" he asked.

For a while Monica sat on the edge of the bed in the moonlight, thinking, remembering a time when she was no older than Benny, and Abbott Fifer had read to her out of the Bible, and had made all the phrases seem like beautiful, stately pictures.

"I know one," she told Benny. "I learned it when I was a little older than you, and I used to say it for my father. It always made me think of trumpets when I said it. Gold and silver trumpets."

"Tell that one," said Benny.

Who shall ascend into the hill of the Lord?
  Or who shall stand in his holy place?

He that hath clean hands and a pure heart,
  Who hath not lifted up his soul unto vanity,
  Nor sworn deceitfully. . . .

Lift up your heads, O ye gates;
Even lift them up, ye everlasting doors;
  And the King of glory shall come in.

Who is this King of glory?

The Lord of hosts,
He is the King of glory.

Benny lay so quietly that Monica thought he was asleep. Cautiously, she eased herself up from the bed and started tiptoeing across the room.

"Monicky?" he called.

"Yes, Benny?"

"If Doak and I get some more pigeons next summer, you know what I'm going to name the female?"

"What?"

"Lady Monicky."

She tiptoed back to the bed, bent over, and kissed him on the cheek.

It was the work of a few moments only for Doak and Benny the next morning to make plans to buy another pair of pigeons the following summer. They would begin saving money right away, they decided. But, once the decision was made, they wandered about disconsolately, thinking of nothing better to do.

"How would you like to put on a play?" proposed Monica. "*Little Red Riding Hood*, maybe. Doak can be the wolf, and Benny can be Little Red Riding Hood."

"Who'll be the grandmother?" asked Benny.

"I'll be the grandmother," offered Nancy.

"And I'll be the mother and start Little Red Riding Hood out with her basket of goodies," said Monica.

"What do we say?" asked Doak.

"Why don't we make a real play of it, Nancy?" suggested Monica. "With costumes and everything?"

"Sure," agreed Nancy. "It'll give us all something to do. I'll make the costumes."

"If we make a play, who's coming to see it?" asked Benny.

"Harlan and Coralie," said Nancy. "And Dad and Mother."

"If we work on it real hard this afternoon," suggested Monica, "do you suppose we can put it on after supper?"

"Why not?" argued Nancy. "We can use the Sociable Porch for a stage. And the audience can sit in the yard."

The rest of the day belonged to Little Red Riding Hood. While Nancy, as if with the touch of a wand, contrived costumes of cast-off clothing, Monica, with suggestions from Doak and Benny as to how a wolf might speak and what he might say, decided on the words for the play. At noon, the four of them carried their lunch to the front yard and spread it on the rustic table in the shade of the maples. As they ate, they talked, and, as they pictured themselves in the roles they were to play, their enthusiasm grew.

"You should organize a company," suggested Uncle Steve, after he and Aunt Willa, Harlan and Coralie had clapped and clapped, and Monica and Nancy had pushed the Wolf and Little Red Riding Hood to the edge of the porch to take a bow. I could look at a play like that every evening."

"Let's do put on another, Monicky," begged Benny. "You don't think so much about pigeons when you're Red Riding Hood."

Throughout the remainder of August, until the week that Monica and Benny were to go home, they gave plays, most of which they adapted from tales they knew—*Hansel and Gretel, Snow White and Rose Red, Gone Is Gone, Rumpelstiltskin,* and *Benjamin West and his Cat Grimalkin.* Feverishly Monica worked on them, fitting together the lines the actors were to say, patiently helping Doak and Benny with their acting, hammering away good-humoredly on details until performances were smooth and lifelike. Feverishly, too, Nancy designed scenery and costumes, and memorized the lines for such roles as were assigned to her.

Doak, as Fritzl in *Gone Is Gone,* so charmed his four spectators with his performance of the old man who thought he'd like to exchange places with his wife that part of the play had to be repeated three times in one evening. And Benny, as Benjamin West, had to carry his cat up to London over and over.

In that way the summer dwindled.

"Why don't we do *Cinderella?*" Nancy asked one night as she and Monica lay in bed discussing the last play they were to give. "Benny would make a sweet Cinderella."

"He would," agreed Monica. "And you'd make a wonderful fairy godmother."

She fell to thinking of Benny, to remembering how, on the night after he lost the pigeons, he had wanted to hear "the kind of stories Uncle Steve reads at bedtime."

"Do you suppose, Nancy," Monica asked, "for our last play we might try something really ambitious?"

"Why not?" laughed Nancy. "We're seasoned actors now. We can tackle almost anything."

"Then let's do a scene from Shakespeare," suggested Monica.

"Shakespeare?" Nancy's tone of voice implied doubt. "I haven't read any of his plays yet, but the kids at school who have to read him groan a lot about it."

"Groan!" exclaimed Monica. "Come to think of it," she added a moment later, "some of them in my school groan, too. But I don't know why. When I was in sixth grade, Daddy read *Macbeth* to me. I didn't understand it, and I did understand it, if you know what I mean. I didn't know all the words, but, the way Daddy read the play, I got their meaning. There are wonderful witches' scenes, and one sleep-walking scene that makes goose flesh break out on you. I memorized all of that scene—Lady Macbeth's part and the doctor's and the nurse's, too. This is the way some of Lady Macbeth's lines go."

She jumped out of bed and ran to the far side of the room. Then, she turned and, striking a pose, advanced haltingly toward Nancy, rubbing her hands as she spoke, and suiting the inflection of her voice to the changes in Lady Macbeth's emotions.

" 'Out, damned spot! Out, I say! One: two: why, then 'tis time to do't. Hell is murky. Fie, my lord, fie! a soldier, and afeard? What need we fear who knows it, when none can call our power to account? Yet who would have thought the old man to have had so much blood in him?' "

"Monica!" cried Nancy. "I've got goose flesh already!"

"Wait! There's more," said Monica, reciting again.

" 'The Thane of Fife had a wife. Where is she now? What,

will these hands ne'er be clean? No more o' that, my lord, no more o' that! You mar all with this starting. . . . Here's the smell of blood still. All the perfumes of Arabia will not sweeten this little hand. Oh, oh, oh!' "

Suddenly she relaxed, and fell back into bed, laughing.

"Well!" declared Nancy. "That part's already assigned. You'll be Lady Macbeth."

"Don't you want that part?" asked Monica. "I can be the nurse. 'I would not have such a heart in my bosom for the dignity of the whole body,'" she recited.

"No!" Nancy was positive. "You're Lady Macbeth. Who else is in the scene? Besides the nurse?"

"Only a doctor."

"Can Doak be the doctor and Benny the nurse?"

"Something tells me," objected Monica, "you have to reach a certain height before you can do Shakespeare."

"Well," said Nancy, "what's wrong with assigning Harlan to be the doctor and Coralie the nurse? They ought to be in one play. Doak and Benny can be knights, or servants, or soldiers standing around with swords, and looking very stiff. They'll like that."

"Especially if you can find some long feathers to put in their hats," agreed Monica. "They can guard Lady Macbeth's door."

The next morning Monica waited for Harlan to come to the barn at milking time to tell him about his assignment, and Coralie's.

"Know what's wrong with you and Nancy?" Harlan laughed. "You don't have enough to do."

"You don't have much to do, either, till it rains," she told him. "I'll copy yours and Coralie's parts off today. And you will do it, Harlan, won't you?"

"When do I memorize?" asked Harlan.

"Any time," said Monica. "All the time. While you're feeding the cattle, or hauling water."

"All right," he said. "You win. I guess a little make-believe around here would help us all."

"Good!" declared Monica. "I'll take the parts to Coralie this morning. And thanks, Harlan."

For four days they worked on the scene. Nancy contrived regal costumes of cast-off clothing and old hat trimmings and cardboard, glue, and poster paint. Doak and Benny, as servants stationed at the entrance to Lady Macbeth's quarters, tried to outdo each other in the length of time they could stand stiffly erect and motionless. Monica, as Lady Macbeth, shut herself up in her bedroom, and recited her lines over and over.

Then came the evening for the performance, the last evening in August, the evening before the day when Monica was to pack to go home.

For Monica, the play was an event to crown all the days of the summer. For as she stood on the Sociable Porch in the twilight, trying piteously to wash the blood from her hands, with Harlan and Coralie watching her from behind a column, and Benny standing stiff and awed on one side and Doak on the other, she knew she had made another discovery. She knew she wanted to act in the plays at school, and she intended reporting for tryouts as soon as they were announced.

Monica and Nancy were a long time getting to bed that night, for there was much to talk about, much to remember. Even after they had turned out the light and had climbed into the old four-poster, they continued to talk.

"Can one person be two people?" asked Monica.

"Dr. Jekyll and Mr. Hyde," Nancy reminded her.

"I'm not Dr. Jekyll and Mr. Hyde," said Monica. "But I know I'm not the Monica you met at the bus that Saturday afternoon in June."

Nancy did not reply for a moment.

"Remember that morning they took T-Bone away, Monica?" she asked, finally. "And I told you you couldn't feel sorry for me because you'd never given up anything? That's the only thing I can think of that's happened all summer I'm really sorry for."

"There's no reason to feel sorry when you tell the truth," Monica said.

"But I didn't tell the truth," said Nancy. "You do feel sorry. I didn't think so then. But now I know you do. And, something else," she went on. "These plays have changed things. The drought is still the drought. But it doesn't seem so bad. I think you've taught me that—that you can reach down inside yourself some place and pull yourself up above anything that happens to you."

"The funny thing is," said Monica thoughtfully, "I don't know that myself. I've never really had to give up, go without, find another way around. I'm not sure I could do that if I had to."

"Of course you could," declared Nancy, generously.

Monica snuggled close to Nancy in bed and put her arm around her.

CHAPTER TEN

The House of the Fifers

September came up the next morning out of the east with undiminished heat, and Monica began packing to go home. As she packed, she entertained a host of ideas, unrelated to each other, but all related to the summer. It might be fun to stay in Kentucky one winter and go to school with Nancy, she thought. Next summer everything would be different on the Fifer farm. Rain would change everything. But rain couldn't wash away the feeling of belonging that possessed her, not if it rained for forty days and forty nights and the Fifers and their animals had to take to an ark. Would Corky be packing now, too, to go to Princeton, she wondered. What would it be like to go to a dance at college? No college dance could ever be quite as thrilling as the square dance in the Colgate High gym. What would Benny grow up to be, she wondered.

To the accompaniment of such reflections, she folded

clothes into her mother's big suitcase, dusted her shoes, tied them in bags, tucked them into the corners of the suitcase, and placed Corky's blue ribbon carefully in one of the pockets.

In the middle of the morning she felt an urge to take one more ride on Firefly, to jog along the roads she knew so well, and look a last time out over the countryside.

As she saddled the mare, she caught sight of Doak and Benny sitting on the edge of the pond back of the barn.

"Hey, kids!" she called. "Want to go?"

"Where're you going?" they asked.

"Nowhere," she answered. "Just for a ride."

"Sure!" they said. They ran down the hill in big, leaping strides, climbed to the top of the barnyard fence, and mounted Firefly, Benny in the middle, Doak behind. Monica clucked, and kicked Firefly's ribs, and with much persuasion started the mare down the lane.

"Why don't we ride to the river," suggested Doak. "We can see if Lance and Gwen have got back yet."

"Sure!" agreed Benny. "It won't hurt to check."

"Well," agreed Monica, "why not? Only," she warned in an attempt to forestall disappointment, "you mustn't really expect to find the pigeons. You might talk to the boy about buying another pair next summer."

More than a month and a half had passed since the three had traveled that road to buy the pigeons. Now, in September, the countryside seemed burned and baked almost beyond the help of the rains that, according to the Fifers, were sure to come any day now.

Doak and Benny, however, talked only of pigeons. The more they talked, and the nearer they came to the house of the boy who had sold them the pigeons, the nearer they came to believing they might find Lancelot and Guinevere waiting for them.

"Thought you folks never was a comin' back," said the boy as they rode up on Firefly.

"Were you expecting us?" asked Monica.

"Sure," he said. "Them pigeons got in just a little bit after you folks left that evenin'."

"What do you mean?" Doak punctuated his question with a heavy thud as he slid off Firefly.

"You mean the pigeons are here?" asked Monica, feeling not altogether certain that she had understood the boy.

"Sure!" he said.

"Why didn't you let us know?" demanded Monica, as she and Benny, too, slid off Firefly.

"I been a meanin' to bring 'em to you, but I never got around to it," explained the boy. "And I kep' a thinkin' you boys'd be right back."

Doak and Benny started sprinting full speed to the stable. Monica and the boy followed behind.

"You would have saved a lot of grief if only you'd let us know the pigeons had come back," she scolded him.

"Well," he said, "looks like, on the other hand, them two'll appreciate 'em all the more, now that they've found 'em again."

They reached the stall and stood looking in at the pigeons. Lancelot and Guinevere, with their necks stiffly arched, their heads resting against their dazzlingly white tails, seemed more haughty than ever.

"You got any way to carry 'em home?" the boy said to Doak and Benny. "I reckon not," he answered his own question. "Won't take but a minute to fix you up."

He brought a crate from the harness room and held the

door open while Doak and Benny caught the pigeons and put them inside.

"You want to take better care of 'em now," he warned. "They mightn't be so obligin' as to come back next time."

"Shucks, man!" declared Doak. "We're going to padlock that door. And if anybody lets 'em out again—"

They mounted Firefly and started home. Never one to hurry, the mare saw no reason for hurrying now, in spite of the fact that Benny and Doak continually kicked her in the ribs, and Monica clucked to her, and slapped her with the reins.

Finding the pigeons after their disappearance so long ago set a pattern that other misfortunes would surely follow, thought Monica. The drought would not last forever. One day rain would fall, and the hold of the drought on the land would be broken. Balbo rye would spring up, the cattle would be fed, and Harlan and Nancy could take up their plans again.

"Hey, Mom!" shouted Doak to Aunt Willa as they rode up to the gate. "Lance and Gwen are home!"

"Can we have a big dinner to celebrate?" called Benny.

Aunt Willa and Nancy came hurrying out of the house. "Where," they asked, "did you find them?"

As Monica began to tell of their adventures, Doak and Benny slid off the mare and started toward the pigeon castle.

"We got to find a padlock, quick," Monica heard Doak saying as he and Benny disappeared around the house.

When Monica had turned Firefly into the barnyard, she walked slowly toward the house, thinking of the good fortune that had befallen the boys. As she stood under the cottonwood tree watching them busily padlocking the door of the old henhouse, she heard Aunt Willa calling to her from the Kinfolks Porch.

"The mail has come, Monica. You have a letter."

Hastily Monica crossed the porch, and took the letter Aunt Willa held out to her.

"From Dad," she said, looking at the envelope.

"Why don't you sit down here on the porch and read it?" invited Aunt Willa.

"Thanks," said Monica. "I'll do that."

As she dropped down on the steps, she noticed that beside Aunt Willa in the swing lay several unopened letters, while in Aunt Willa's lap lay the opened pages of still another letter. Suddenly it struck her that there had been a note of concern in Aunt Willa's voice.

She studied her own letter apprehensively.

"Aunt Willa," she asked, "has something happened?"

Thoughtfully Aunt Willa fingered the letter that lay in her lap.

"No, Monica," she said, her voice tender with kindness. "I have a letter from your father, too," she added.

Monica, glancing at Aunt Willa's face anxiously, tore open the envelope of her own letter, and began to read. Hurriedly her eyes followed the lines across the first page.

Suddenly she stopped reading and looked at Aunt Willa.

"It's not fair!" she declared, swallowing hard. Tears came into her eyes. She covered her face with the letter and began to cry. "It's not fair at all!" she sobbed. "Why is he doing it?"

Aunt Willa was silent a moment before interrupting Monica's outburst.

"You haven't read all your father's letter yet, child," she

said gently to Monica. "I expect he tells you on the other page why he's doing it. Read it all. Then we'll talk about it."

"Did he tell you?" sobbed Monica.

"Yes, dear."

"Then you tell me. I can't bear to read it," she begged.

Again Aunt Willa was silent a moment before replying. Finally she asked, "Do you know Ruth Hunter, Monica?"

Monica wiped her eyes and swallowed hard. "Yes," she said in a tear-choked voice. "She's a teacher at home. I've known her all—all my life. She was one of Mother's best friends."

"From what your father tells me, she is a very fine person," Aunt Willa said.

"What else did he tell you?" demanded Monica. In the quiet summer morning her voice shouted.

"Your father and Ruth have a great deal in common, Monica," said Aunt Willa. "They both love a home. They both enjoy friends and books and music and children. It was natural that their friendship should grow into love, and that they should want to make a home together."

"When are they—marrying?" demanded Monica, tearfully.

"Don't you want to read your own letter?" asked Aunt Willa. "I imagine your father has told you everything."

As Monica glanced at the letter, her sobs began anew. She flung the letter on the floor.

"I can't read it, Aunt Willa!" she cried. "I can't!"

"They're going to be married sometime this fall, my dear," Aunt Willa told her. "After you return home and they can talk everything over with you."

To Monica, life seemed abruptly stopped. She buried her face against her knees and cried brokenheartedly.

"It's all right, my dear," she heard Aunt Willa saying after a while, soothingly. "Ruth Hunter must be the kind of woman who will make a real home for your father and for you. She'll make things easier, and much happier for you both, if you'll let her. She'd have to be that kind of woman else your father would never have loved her and wanted to share you with her."

Monica heard the words Aunt Willa said as if they were spoken in a great void. Her world—her safe, secure world of which she had been the center—had been blown to pieces.

"It means rearranging your life, my dear," went on Aunt Willa, reading Monica's thoughts, "but it's best for everybody, child."

Monica tried to answer her, but she couldn't speak. She felt as if somebody had knocked the breath out of her, and no air could reach her lungs. She managed to get to her feet, and, with her letter in her hand, she stumbled blindly toward the door.

"Take your letter up to your room, won't you," said Aunt Willa, "and read it? Your father wanted to tell you about this himself."

Monica jerked the door open, and went into the house and up the stairs. Then she slammed her bedroom door and fell sobbing across the bed.

Later, she came down to lunch when Aunt Willa called her, her eyes swollen and red with crying. Doak and Benny were awed by her appearance and respected her grief by keeping silent. Nancy and Uncle Steve, when they spoke to her, seemed wanting to get under her grief and help her bear it. But Aunt Willa insisted on talking about Ruth Hunter, and about the fact that she was going to marry

Abbott Fifer, as if it were not only a natural event, but a wonderfully happy one, too.

"Monica," she said when they were washing dishes, "I think you ought to send your father and Ruth a telegram."

"Should I say in it what I think?" blurted Monica, and immediately the tears began to flow again as she made for the stairs.

It was the middle of the afternoon before she could control herself, before she could rouse herself to face a situation from which she knew there could be no running away. Before the mirror she brushed her hair and powdered her nose. Then, she came down the stairs in search of Aunt Willa. She remembered how good, how safe, it had seemed to sound off to Aunt Willa whenever she couldn't understand, or couldn't follow the Fifers. Now, perhaps, if she could sound off once more, get some of the bitterness and disappointment out of her system—

Aunt Willa was writing a letter on the Kinfolks Porch. Her hands relaxed in her lap as Monica appeared.

"Yes, my dear?" she asked.

Instead of sounding off as she had intended, Monica spread her hands beseechingly, and asked as the tears started afresh, "Aunt Willa, what do I do?"

"Can you hear me if I speak to you, Monica?" Aunt Willa asked gently.

Monica blew her nose hard, wiped her eyes, and nodded her head.

"I'll try," she said, swallowing hard.

"What's happened is, in a sense, like a play that you might be putting on," said Aunt Willa. "But you aren't directing this. Somebody else is directing it. You're one of the actors. In this particular scene, you're the main actor.

You're cast in the role of a grown-up, Monica. You're no longer a child who wants to continue to be the center of her father's life and affection, but a grown-up daughter who loves her father and senses his needs, and wants him to be happy, and is willing to do her share to make him happy. It's a hard role to play, Monica. But you can do it."

"But what do I say?" wailed Monica. "Nobody has written any lines for me to say."

"You write your own lines," Aunt Willa told her, "as you go along. From one day to the next. From one scene to the next."

More hot tears splashed down Monica's cheeks before she could control her emotions. Finally, she wiped her eyes, leaned her head against a porch pillar, and looked at the sky. She noticed vaguely that clouds were piling up in the west.

"You could say your first lines in a telegram, Monica," suggested Aunt Willa. "Nothing could be more fitting than to send your father and Ruth a grown-up telegram of love and congratulations. They're as anxious about your happiness as you are. That's why they're waiting to talk things over with you."

"I know, Aunt Willa," Monica agreed, her voice still plaintive. "I know the words are right. But I don't feel their meanings. I can't say words when I don't feel their meanings."

"Sometimes loving a little is all you need to persuade your feelings to go in the direction you know they ought to go," Aunt Willa told her.

Still Monica continued to stare off into the sky.

"How would you like to write out a telegram and have me phone it in?" asked Aunt Willa. "Here's pen and paper."

Monica took the paper and pen. After many false starts, she wrote a message, counted the words, and handed it to her aunt.

"That's good, my dear," said Aunt Willa as she read it. "That's acting your role very well."

She went into the house and dialed the phone.

"Wait a minute, Aunt Willa!" called Monica as she jerked open the screen door. "I'll phone it in."

Monica had looked forward to a festive last evening in the house of the Fifers. And Aunt Willa did what she could to make it festive for her. She prepared Monica's favorite dishes, and invited Harlan and Coralie to supper. But Monica found it hard to enter into the festivity. She felt herself an onlooker, not an active participant. It was hard, even, for her to enter into the conversation. She soon lapsed into silence and listened to Harlan report on his plans for sowing Balbo rye. Disking the fields now was about like disking a concrete pavement, Harlan said.

In the late evening, as Uncle Steve took up the Bible to read, Monica settled herself expectantly in her chair. She knew now why Benny, in the night after he had lost the pigeons, wanted to hear a "story" such as Uncle Steve read from the Bible. Uncle Steve's voice, to which she was aware she was listening for the last time during the summer, seemed unusually rich, and comforting, and healing.

O Lord, thou hast searched me, and known me.
Thou knowest my downsitting and mine uprising,
Thou understandest my thought afar off.
Thou compassest my path and my lying down,
and art acquainted with all my ways. . . .
Search me, O God, and know my heart;

try me, and know my thoughts,
and see if there be any wicked way in me,
and lead me in the way everlasting.

Monica had imagined, too, that once in bed, she and Nancy would talk into the small hours. But talk in bed with Nancy came no easier than talk had come at the dinner table. After Nancy had made a few unrewarded efforts, she turned over in bed and went to sleep.

Monica, however, could not sleep. She lay awake in the darkness, thinking, remembering. She was no longed ruffled, distraught. The sending of the telegram had had something to do with that, she realized. The moment she had sent the telegram, her mind had started clearing.

Leisurely the summer passed in review before her memory, with here and there a bit of conversation, a mood, or a discovery lingering for a moment to be relived in the light of this thing that had happened to her.

She could hear Nancy's voice as it had come to her from that very bed—"Oh, go away! You never had to give up anything in your life!" Now she was giving up something. Like Nancy, like all the drought-stricken young people, she was being forced to adjust to a new way of life by some circumstance beyond her control. Now, at last, she understood.

But surely, she chided herself, she was not giving up as much as Nancy had given up. This thing that had happened to her—it wasn't the sort of calamity that had befallen Nancy.

She pondered this matter as she lay in the darkness. No, she told herself, her father's marriage was no calamity that had befallen her, that had caused her so much grief. Her distress was born rather of the knowledge that her old relationships were changed beyond recall, and that she must adjust to a new pattern, enlarge her thinking to include Ruth Hunter, "love a little," as Aunt Willa had told her. The circumstances that came to people, like uninvited and permanent visitors, were never the same, she decided. It was the fact of having to adjust to whatever visitors came that made the world kin, she decided. It was that that helped her to understand Nancy.

And this ability finally to understand—wasn't it an achievement like learning to milk, learning to make a dress, learning to drive a car, learning that in earning her self-respect she earned the respect of other people as well? Maybe learning to understand was the achievement that crowned them all, she thought with satisfaction.

Quietly she stole out of bed and went to kneel by the window where she had knelt weeks ago to listen to the whippoorwill. No whippoorwill sang now, however, nor cattle bawled, nor dog barked. No stars spangled the sky, she noticed. The earth was totally dark. The shapes of the familiar hills and valleys she could nowhere make out. Yet how distinct they were in her mind, how clear in her memory, how somehow loved!

She thought of Corky, and of the dance to which he was going to invite her in the fall. What would Corky think of her afternoon's performance, she wondered, of her giving way so completely to her unhappiness? Corky would be ashamed of her, she decided. Still, she comforted herself, Corky would be proud to see her climbing out of her tailspin as she knew she was doing now.

She remembered the strange homesickness that had enveloped her that other night she had knelt by the window listening to the whippoorwill. Some inner order—that was the thing she had craved; some wholeness, some perfectness that could soar strong and free, like the song of the whippoorwill. And now, in some small measure, she sensed that order within herself. Even though she had temporarily lost her balance, she knew now that she had regained it. And, what was more, she intended to keep it.

Quietly she started back to bed again, feeling in the darkness the broad braids of Nancy's rag rug under her bare feet. She paused a moment in front of the place where she calculated Great-aunt Eugenia's picture would be hanging. There had never been judgment of her in Great-aunt Eugenia's eyes, she knew now. There was only the love of being young shining in them, and the liveliness of understanding.

Suddenly, all of Monica's heart went out to the young girl in the portrait—she who at seventeen was killed by a fall from a horse just when she was about to be married.

A long time Monica stood, remembering, feeling the summer in the house of the Fifers, with all of its dark and all of its shining moments, shaping into one satisfying, healing whole.

Back in bed, she recalled all that Aunt Willa had said to her about the house of the Fifers on the day they drove into Colgate for the zinnia plants and the learner's permit. The old house had known many storms, Aunt Willa had said. But it had weathered them all.

For a hundred years, Monica calculated, the Fifer house had weathered its storms. Some of them, like Great-aunt Eugenia's death and the debt-encumbering drought, had been tragic storms. But the house of the Fifers was still standing, sturdy and unmoved by disaster. Moreover, she was a Fifer, too, and the tradition of the old house was in her blood. It was good, she realized, to have in her heritage a tradition of sturdiness, of remaining steadfast through whatever storms that might beat upon her and blow her off her course.

After a time she was aware of a sound on the roof—a dry, rattling sound as of nuts being poured from a bag. She raised her head and listened.

Rain! Rain was falling on the roof. It came in small gusts on the wind and receded as if on hurrying feet, and then came again. It wasn't the drenching rain the parched earth needed. But it was a promise of more rain to come. The drought would now be broken. Harlan's fall pasture would spring up. The ponds would fill with water.

The next morning, Aunt Willa and Uncle Steve, Nancy, Doak, and Benny went with Monica to the bus. The sky was overcast, and the cooled air smelled of rain. On the Roller Coaster Road they met Harlan on the tractor, hauling a disk harrow to one of the west fields to begin preparing a seedbed for Balbo rye. At sight of them, Harlan's face broke into a great smile such as Monica had not seen all summer. Snatching his old straw hat from his head, he waved it broadly.

"By, Monicky!" he shouted. "Be seeing you next summer!"

As the car topped the last of the roller-coaster hills before the highway, Monica turned and took a last look at the old Fifer house, standing serenely on its knoll among the silver maples. She gazed at it until she could see it no more. She wanted to carry the shape of it in her heart against the days of adjustment ahead.

Waiting for the bus that morning was like waiting for all buses. Everyone had things to say, and no one could remember at the moment what they were.

As the bus pulled around the corner and eased up to the filling station, Aunt Willa put her arm around Monica.

"All the Fifers want you to come back next summer, Monica," she said, a ring of sincerity in her voice. "Corky, Benny, all of us."

"I want to come," Monica said simply. But she remembered how adamant her father had been about sending her this summer. He might be just as adamant about keeping her home another summer. "If Daddy will let me," she added.

The driver stepped down from the bus and waited for the passengers to alight.

"You have a right, Monica," Aunt Willa said, "to help decide what you shall do. You earned the right this summer."

"If I have any say about it, then," said Monica, "I'll be back. Do you know what I'd like to do, Aunt Willa? I'd like to collect all the stories you and Uncle Steve know of all the Fifers who ever lived in our old house."

"Say!" said Nancy. "That gives me an idea. We could make them into a play."

"Show your tickets, please," commanded the driver as he stationed himself at the bus door.

"Don't lose your ticket, now, Monica," cautioned Doak.

"If Monicky does," said Benny, "she'll earn money to buy another."

All the Fifers laughed. In a quick impulse, Nancy threw her arms about Monica.

"Tickets, please!" said the driver.

Monica, half-laughing, half-crying, showed him her ticket. She stepped aboard and found a seat by a window. Opening the air slots, she called out to the Fifers, "I'll be seeing you next summer."